Can a boy and a dragon be friends?

THE DRAGONLING COLLECTOR'S EDITION, VOL. 2

Dragons of Krad

Krad is even more dangerous than Darek had expected. Can he rescue his friends?

Dragon Trouble

Darek, Pola, and Rowena know that their fathers are now in terrible danger. How will they escape from Krad?

Dragons and Kings

A power-hungry tyrant has taken over Darek's village. Now he and his dragon are going to war!

The Dragonling series
by Jackie French Koller

THE DRAGONLING COLLECTOR'S EDITION, Vol. 1
    The Dragonling
    A Dragon in the Family
    Dragon Quest

THE DRAGONLING COLLECTOR'S EDITION, Vol. 2
    Dragons of Krad
    Dragon Trouble
    Dragons and Kings

The
Dragonling

COLLECTOR'S EDITION

VOL. 2

DRAGONS OF KRAD ♦ DRAGON TROUBLE ♦ DRAGONS AND KINGS

JACKIE FRENCH KOLLER

A MINSTREL® BOOK

Published by POCKET BOOKS
New York   London   Toronto   Sydney   Singapore

To my brother, Jim, with love.

A Minstrel Paperback published by
POCKET BOOKS, a division of Simon & Schuster, Inc.
1230 Avenue of the Americas, New York, NY 10020

Dragons of Krad copyright © 1997 by Jackie French Koller
Dragon Trouble copyright © 1997 by Jackie French Koller
Dragons and Kings copyright © 1998 by Jackie French Koller

ISBN: 0-7434-1020-3

First Minstrel Books printing January 2001

10 9 8 7 6 5 4 3 2 1

A MINSTREL BOOK and colophon are registered trademarks of Simon & Schuster, Inc.

Front cover illustrations by Judith Mitchell

Printed in the U.S.A.

These titles were previously published individually by Minstrel Books.

Dragons
of Krad

Prologue

When Darek rescued a baby dragon and brought it home to his village, he dreamed of a bright new tomorrow where dragons and Zorians could live together as friends. And indeed, after a difficult beginning, Darek and his dragon, Zantor, did win the hearts of the villagers.

But Darek didn't count on the jealousy of the other Zorian children. Rowena, daughter to the Chief Elder, grew to love Zantor deeply. When Darek refused to allow her to play with Zantor, Rowena begged her father for a dragonling of her own. This wish sparked a dragon quest that ended in tragedy. Darek's best friend, Pola, along with Zantor and three other Great Blue dragonlings, were lost when a runaway wagon carried them into the dreaded Black Mountains of Krad.

Filled with grief and rage, Darek confronted Rowena and blamed her for the tragedy. Determined to right the wrongs she had done, Rowena slipped away in the night on a quest to find Pola and the dragons. When Darek discovered that she was headed for the Black Mountains, he followed, bent on stopping her. But Rowena would not be stopped. Instead, she helped Darek to see that they both shared the blame for the tragedy.

Now the two have discovered that they share something else—the ability to communicate with Zantor. While they are arguing, a mind message comes from the dragonling—a cry for help. Putting aside past differences, Darek and Rowena set off on a new quest. Together they venture into the Black Mountains, risking everything to find their friends.

1

Dark mists swirled around Darek as he made his way up a narrow pass into the Black Mountains of Krad. Rowena, daughter of the Zorian Chief Elder, followed a few steps behind. The mist felt damp against Darek's skin, and the stench of it made him gag. It smelled like rotted burning flesh, and that worried him.

Darek heard a cough and looked back over his shoulder.

"Are you all right?" he asked.

"Yes." Rowena nodded. "I'm getting tired,

though. My eyes sting, and it's hard to breathe."

"Shall we rest awhile?" Darek asked.

"No. Pola and Zantor may be in danger. We've got to keep going."

Darek nodded. He could hear the mind cries, too. His dragon friend, Zantor, was sending messages of distress. Zantor and Darek's best friend, Pola, had disappeared into the Black Mountains more than a week ago. They and three other Great Blue dragonlings had been carried off by a runaway wagon. Darek and Rowena felt responsible. They had been jealous of each other and had quarreled over Zantor. As a result, the Chief Elder had ordered his men to capture another dragonling for Rowena. While on the dragon quest, Pola, Zantor, and the others had been lost.

Rowena coughed again and gasped for air.

"Pull your collar up over your mouth and nose," Darek said. "The cloth will filter some of the smoke."

Strange shapes loomed out of the mist. Black

rocks, like cinders, dotted their path. All of Darek's senses were alert, keen to the dangers that might assail them at any moment.

"I wonder what our families will think when they wake this morning and find us gone," he said quietly.

Rowena didn't answer right away.

"We must not think of that," she said at last. "We must dream of the day when we return with Pola and the dragons."

Darek wished he could be sure that day would come, but he could not. No one had ever returned from the Black Mountains of Krad. For centuries now, it had been forbidden even to venture into them. What would his parents and his older brother, Clep, think when they realized where he had gone? He could see his mother's tearstained face now.

We will find a way back, Mother, he promised silently.

"Did you hear that?" Rowena suddenly cried out.

Darek stopped and listened. He thought he heard a soft scuffling sound, but when he peered into the mist, all he could make out were strange, twisted rock forms and the stumps of long-dead trees. "I don't see anything," he whispered.

"No," Rowena said. "I guess not." She put her hand to her forehead and moaned softly. "Ooohh," she said. "My head and stomach ache."

Darek's head hurt, too. Could the very mists be poisonous? he wondered.

"We're almost to the peak," he told Rowena. "It will be easier going down the other side. We won't have to breathe as hard."

The ground beneath them leveled off at long last, and they started to descend. Darek began to move with greater caution. If something or someone was waiting below, he wanted to see it before it saw him. His headache was worse, making it harder and harder to think. Behind him, he heard Rowena moan once more.

"Are you sure you're all right?" he asked again.

"Yes," she said, but her voice trembled.

Darek's worry deepened. He had to get her out of the mountains quickly. "Can you walk any faster?" he asked.

"I—I don't know. I can't even think straight."

Darek turned. Rowena's skin was very pale, and her lips looked blue.

"Lean on me," he said.

Rowena gladly took his arm, and they struggled on together. Darek shook his head. It felt as if the mist were seeping into his mind. Minutes seemed to drag by. Rowena was leaning on him more and more heavily.

"Is it much farther?" she asked weakly.

"No, not much. See, the mist is thinning."

"Good, because I don't feel . . . ooohh." Rowena suddenly pushed Darek aside, clapped a hand over her mouth, and started to run.

Darek stumbled on a cinder and fell. "Rowena, wait!" he cried. He scrambled to his feet again, but before he could catch her, Rowena disappeared into the mist.

"Rowena!" he called, but there was no reply, only a distant retching sound.

Then, suddenly, there was a scream.

2

Darek fought the urge to run in the direction of the scream. Instead, he moved cautiously, stealing from rock to rock. If someone, or something, had caught Rowena, he had to be careful. It would do neither of them any good if he got captured, too. The mist had cleared a little, and he could begin to see something of Krad. It was a bleak, colorless place, with runty, withered trees and stubby brown grasses.

A movement below caught his eye, and he strained to see.

11

Rowena!

His friend had reached the plateau at the foot of the mountains. There she was surrounded by a number of bent little creatures that hopped about her excitedly. They were chanting over and over in high, flutelike voices.

"A pretty!" they cried. "A pretty! A pretty!"

Rowena hugged her arms around her like a frightened child. "Go away! Go away!" she cried. "Leave me alone!"

Before long, there was another sound— hooves pounding in the distance. Darek looked toward the horizon and saw a group of riders thunder up over the lip of the plateau. The riders were broad and tall, with dark, hooded capes. They were mounted on long-haired white yukes, much like the ones back in Zoriak, only larger. As the riders bore down on Rowena, the little bent creatures around her shrieked and scurried away.

One of the smaller ones was too slow. A whip lashed out from the hand of one of the riders

and stung it a fierce blow on the leg. The creature yelped and scrabbled into the brush. The rider threw his head back and laughed. His hood fell away, and Darek saw a face that was humanlike but covered in fur.

A Kraden!

A chill crept up Darek's back. Back in Zoriak, he had heard stories of Kradens—big, hairy men who had supposedly driven the Zorians out of Krad long ago. Darek had always thought they were just old tales. But these Kradens were real—living and breathing! Poor Rowena looked terrified.

"Who are you?" one of the Kradens demanded.

"Rowena," she answered in a trembling voice.

"Why have you come here?" the man asked.

Rowena seemed at a loss to answer.

Darek felt confused, too. Why *had* they come there? Had the mist addled his mind? Why couldn't he remember?

Then he heard a sound deep inside his head. *Rrronk!* Yes! Zantor. Zantor and Pola. That was why they had come. He must keep focused on that.

Rowena must have heard the mind cry, too. "My friends!" she said suddenly. "They're in trouble. I've come to help them."

"Have you, now?" The men looked at one another and chuckled. "And how is a slip of a girl like you going to help anyone?"

Rowena drew herself up and tossed her head. "I'm stronger than I look," she announced.

At this, all the men burst out laughing.

"That's good news," one of them said, "because we've plenty of work for you to do."

Rowena crossed her arms. "Work?" she said. "I'll not work for you. I'm the daughter of the Chief Elder."

"Are you, now?" another Kraden said. "Well, then, we'll have to find you a jewel-handled broom, won't we?"

With another loud laugh, the Kradens swooped forward, and one of them scooped Rowena up, pulling her into his saddle.

"Come, lads," he said. "Let's take *Her Highness* to visit old Jazee." Then he and the others turned their yukes around and thundered away.

Darek stared after them. Who was old Jazee? he wondered. And what did the man mean when he said there was plenty of work to do? It did not bode well.

Darek decided to try to keep his own presence a secret until he could learn more. Slowly, he crept down the mountainside until he reached the place where Rowena had been captured. He noticed a trail of dark droplets among the footprints and remembered the small creatures and the lash of the whip. Suddenly, he heard a high, thin cry.

"Gleeep. Gleeep."

Darek's head jerked around. The wounded creature was lying beside a nearby rock, nursing its leg. It caught sight of him and scrambled to

get away, but it was only able to move a few steps before collapsing again.

"Gellp!" it cried.

Darek frowned. He had no time to help a wounded . . . whatever. He started to walk away, but his conscience would not let him. Quickly, he pulled his shirt out of his britches and tore a strip from the hem. Then he unfastened the water skin from his belt and squirted a little into the dirt at his feet, mixing a muddy paste. Taking a handful of the paste, he approached the creature. It shrank back, staring at him with huge yellow-green eyes.

"I won't hurt you," Darek soothed. "I just want to help." He knelt beside the creature and gently straightened its leg.

"Gellp!" it cried again.

"Sorry," Darek said. "This should make you feel better." The creature was the size of a young child, with scaly gray skin. It looked almost like a cross between a dragon and a human. Darek couldn't help feeling kindly toward it. He packed the healing mud over the wound, then gently bandaged the leg.

"There," Darek said, getting to his feet again. "If you stay off it for a day or two, you should be fine."

The creature turned and pointed a knobby finger toward the road. "Your pretty?" it asked.

Darek looked down the road, too. There was no sign of Rowena or the men now. "No," he answered. "She's not my pretty. But she's my friend. Do you know where they've taken her?"

"Zahr take pretty," the creature said.

"Zahr?" Darek said. "Who's Zahr?"

The creature gave a little cough. "Zahr, king," it said hoarsely.

Darek stared again at the empty road. "Where did Zahr take pretty?" he asked.

"Slave camp," the creature said.

Darek whirled around. "Slave camp! What do you mean, slave camp?"

The creature cringed. "Go now," it said, scrambling away.

"No, wait." Darek took a breath to calm himself. "Please tell me more about the slave camp," he pleaded.

The creature coughed again. "Go now," it repeated. And then, almost magically, it disappeared.

"Hey, wait!" Darek called after it. "One more question, please! Have you seen another Zorian, like me, or a small blue dragon?"

"Zahhhr," came the faint, choked reply.

3

Darting from tree to scrubby tree, Darek slowly made his way across the plateau. The mist was thinner now, and his head seemed to be clearing. In the distance, he heard fearful, roaring sounds. Cautiously, he approached the lip where he had first seen the Kradens. He got down on his belly, inched forward, and peered out across the valley. A large, rambling village stretched in front of him. It had a grim look to it. A gray, smoke-stained castle stood at its center. This was surrounded by smaller houses and

hundreds of squat stone hovels. The mist, though thin, hung over everything. Suddenly, Darek heard a roar just below him. He looked down, and his breath caught in his throat.

"Zatz!" he swore softly.

There at the base of the plateau was a huge cage, nearly half the size of the town. Great creatures milled about in it, roaring and belching flame at one another.

Red Fanged dragons!

Darek had never seen a Red Fanged dragon before. The last one in Zoriak had been killed long before he was born. He knew all about them from legends, though. They were not red, as their name might suggest, but pearly white. Quite beautiful, actually, were it not for the vicious red fangs that gave their mouths the look of dripping blood. It was not just their looks that made them fearsome, though. They were also huge, second only in size to the Great Blues. And they were flesh lovers. Reds dined mostly on other dragons, but in Zoriak they had been known to raid the village from time to time.

Darek shuddered at the thought. He stared down at the cage again. How much meat must it take to satisfy the appetites of so many Red Fanged dragons? he wondered. Portions of charred dragon skeletons lay strewn about the pen, and a steady stream of smoke rose up from it. Red Fanged dragons always flamed their prey alive before eating it. So this was the source of the mist, Darek suddenly realized. Dragons-breath!

Why would the Kradens keep these beasts? he wondered.

"Well, well!" A loud voice startled Darek. "What have we here?"

Darek looked up and saw a dark, hooded figure towering over him. He started to scramble to his knees, but something hard and sharp dug into his back and pressed him to the dirt.

"Not so fast, Zorian!" the voice commanded.

Darek slowly twisted to get a better look at

the figure. A thick, metal-encrusted boot was planted near his shoulder. Darek's gaze followed it up. A large, furry-faced man stared down at him.

"State your name and mission," the man snarled.

Darek tried to keep his voice from trembling. "Darek," he said. "Darek of Zoriak. Some . . . some of my friends fled into these mountains a few days back. I . . . I'm only trying to find them."

The Kraden laughed. "Another one?" he said. "What sorts of fools are the Zorians raising these days?"

Darek did not answer.

"Well," the Kraden said, "no matter. Fresh blood is always welcome here."

The Kraden lifted the lance from between Darek's shoulders and plunged it into the dust not a finger's breadth from his nose.

"On your feet!" he bellowed.

Darek scrambled to do as he was told. He

stood straight and tall. Still, he only came up to the man's middle.

The Kraden glared down at him, pulling on his hairy chin. "How old are you?" he asked.

"A Decanum," Darek said.

The Kraden shook his head and swore. "Too young for the mines," he grumbled. "You any good with dragons?"

"Yes, sir," Darek said, swallowing hard again. "But . . . I don't plan to stay."

At this, the Kraden threw his head back and roared. He laughed until tears rolled down his furry cheeks. Then he slapped his leg and laughed some more.

"Don't plan to stay . . ." he repeated breathlessly when at last he could speak again. "That's a good one, lad. A good one indeed."

Then his eyes narrowed, and his lips twisted into a sneer. "No one ever leaves Krad," he growled.

4

Castle Krad was as dark and forbidding up close as it had looked from afar. Darek stared at its twisted, smoke-stained battlements.

"Is that where Zahr lives?" he asked.

The Kraden's eyes narrowed.

"Where did you hear the name of Zahr?" he asked.

"A little creature told me," Darek said, "back on the mountain. He said Zahr had taken my friends."

The Kraden's brows crashed together.

"Blasted Zynots," he swore. "What else did they tell you?"

Darek shook his head. "Nothing," he said.

The Kraden eyed him suspiciously. "Well, no matter," he said. "That's all you'll remember soon enough—nothing." He pushed open the heavy door of a low stone house and motioned Darek inside.

It was steamy and dark inside and smelled of medicines and herbs. It took a few moments for Darek's eyes to adjust to the dimness. Then he

was able to make out an old cronelike woman bent over the hearth.

"Another customer for you, Jazee," the man said.

The woman looked up in surprise. "Another?" she said. "That's three in a fortnight!"

Darek's ears perked up. Three! He and Rowena were two. The third must have been Pola!

"Aye." The man nodded. "This one thinks he's here on holiday. Told me he's not staying."

The crone cackled. "Jazee will cure him of that," she said. She picked up one of her vials and poured a few drops of green liquid into a carved stone cup. "Drink up, boy," she said.

Darek pressed his lips tight and turned away.

"Do as Jazee says," the man growled. He grabbed Darek and pulled his mouth open. The crone poured the liquid down his throat. It burned and made him gag. When he looked at the woman again, he felt lightheaded and dizzy. He tried to look away, but her eyes held his fast.

"Tell me who you are," she commanded.

"Darek," Darek mumbled. The woman's face wavered and swam before his eyes.

"Darek who?" the crone asked.

Darek searched inside his head for an answer, but his mind was nothing but a vast, empty cave. "I . . . don't know."

The woman smiled. "You are Darek of Krad," she told him, "slave to the Kingdom of Zahr. From your past life, you will remember only the things that are of use to us here. Go now with Org and do as you are commanded."

5

Darek followed Org through narrow, twisted, foul-smelling streets. Kraden children hissed and spat at him. Women leaned out of the doorways and called him names like "dragon-wit" and "fang-breath." It was a relief at last to reach the pastures at the far side of town. Vast numbers of dragons grazed there, but not the Red Fangs. They were kept in their cage on the outskirts of the village. Darek recognized some of the dragons—Green Horned, Yellow Crested, and Purple Spotted. Others were new to him.

"You'll know all there is to know of dragons before long," Org told him.

Darek was not unhappy at this prospect. The dragons were far more pleasant, it seemed, than the people of Krad. But why were the great creatures content to stay among such men?

"Why don't the dragons just fly away?" he asked Org.

"They can't," Org told him. "We bind their wings when they're young, until their flight muscles wither. You'll see soon enough. Come. Might as well get you started."

Darek followed Org into a long, low building. It was a combination stable and nursery for the dragons, as well as a dormitory for the slaves who tended them. A number of slaves were hard at work mucking out the dragon stalls. They looked up when Darek and Org came in. Darek felt an immediate kinship with them. They were not large and furry like the Kradens. They looked much like Darek and seemed close to him in age, too. The slaves paused and stared as Darek and

Org passed, but the crack of an overseer's whip quickly returned them to their duties.

"Got a new one for you, Daxon," Org said, pushing Darek toward another Kraden.

The man named Daxon seemed pleased. "Three in a fortnight," he said, raising his eyebrows. "To what do we owe this good fortune?"

Org shrugged. "Word must be spreading about the pleasures of life here in Krad."

Daxon roared with laughter over this joke.

Org grabbed Darek by the collar and shoved him in front of Daxon. "Bow," he said, pushing Darek to his knees. "Daxon is master of the stockyards, your master now, too. You will call him Master when you speak to him, and you will obey his orders without question." Then he let Darek go and turned to face Daxon.

"His name is Darek," he said. "Jazee probed his thoughts. She says he should be a natural with dragons. Rebellious by nature, though, so don't spare the whip."

Daxon laughed. "When have you ever known me to spare the whip, my friend?" He looked down at Darek, pulling at the fur on his chin. "Rebellious, huh?" he said slowly. "Well, we'll just have to see to it that you're too tired to rebel, won't we?" Daxon looked over toward the other slaves. "Pola!" he shouted. "Come here!"

One of the slaves dropped his rake and hurried over. Darek couldn't help noticing how thin and tired the boy looked. His hands were all raw and blistered. The slave bowed to Daxon.

"Yes, Master?" he said.

"Take this new slave and teach him everything you've learned. Start in the nursery. No supper for either of you until the pens are cleaned, the dragonlings fed, and the newborns wing-bound."

Pola's face fell. "Yes, Master," he whispered, bowing again. Then to Darek he said, "Follow me."

Darek rose to follow, but suddenly Daxon's

hand flew out and boxed his ear. "Bow!" he thundered.

Darek quickly dipped his head. "Yes, Master," he mumbled.

"That's better," Daxon said. "Never enter or leave my presence without bowing!"

Darek bowed once more, just to be safe, then turned and silently followed Pola.

6

A million questions raced through Darek's mind as he followed Pola along the corridor to the nursery. He hoped he and this slave boy would have a chance to talk privately. Maybe Pola could help him understand what was happening to him.

"Here," Pola said. He took a rake down from a hook on the wall and handed it to Darek. Then he pushed a door open and motioned Darek through.

The air inside was warm and damp and filled

with the chirpings and callings of young dragons. Darek couldn't help smiling at the colorful creatures, tumbling and playing on the nursery floor. He noticed a little cluster of Blues huddled together, sleeping, on the far side of the room. His smile broadened. They were so beautiful, even as babies. But the bandages wound tightly around their silvery wings saddened Darek.

"How long do they have to wear those things?" he asked.

"Half an anum," Pola said tiredly. "Until their wing muscles shrink beyond repair."

"Why don't the Kradens want them to fly?" Darek asked.

"They're easier to manage this way," Pola said.

"Who *are* these Kradens?" Darek began. "And why . . ."

"Look," Pola interrupted. "We've got a lot of work ahead of us if we want to eat."

Just then, Darek heard a commotion. He looked and saw that one of the little Blues had awakened. It was struggling to make its way through the maze of other dragons toward Darek and Pola.

"Thrummm!" Darek could hear it singing as it got closer. *"Thrummm, thrummm, thrummm."* Darek could have sworn its big green eyes were looking right at him.

Pola frowned. "That dratted Blue," he said. "Too darn friendly for its own good."

The Blue dragon kept making little hops in a sad attempt to fly. But that, of course, was impossible. At last, it hurled itself through the air and smacked with a thud into Darek's chest. Both of them tumbled to the ground.

"Thrummm," the dragonling sang. *"Thrummm, thrummm, thrummm."* Then *thwip, thwip!* Out flicked its forked tongue, covering Darek with tickly kisses.

Darek twisted and rolled, laughing until his stomach hurt.

"Stop it! Hey!" he begged. "What's wrong with you, you silly thing?" He finally managed

to push the beast off and get back to his feet. Still, the creature kept dancing around him, butting him and nuzzling his chest.

"He seems to want something in your jerkin pocket," Pola said.

"There isn't anything in my pocket," Darek said. He put his arms up to fend off another nuzzle.

"He sure seems to think there is," Pola said.

"Well, there isn't," Darek insisted. But he felt his pocket just to be sure.

There *was* something there. Darek reached in and pulled out several hard, white lumps.

"*Thrummm,*" sang the little dragon. It gobbled the lumps before Darek even got a good look at them.

"What were they?" Pola asked.

"I don't know," Darek said. "But *he* sure seemed to know. I wonder how?"

Pola shrugged. "Smell?"

Darek shook his head. "Dragons don't have much sense of smell."

The little dragon nuzzled Darek's pocket once more. "Sorry, pal," Darek said with a laugh. "I don't have any more." He rubbed the budding horns on the dragon's head.

"I wouldn't do that if I were you," Pola warned.

"Do what?" Darek asked.

"Get too friendly with him. It'll just make it harder in the end."

"In the end?" Darek repeated. "What do you mean?"

"When they feed him to the Red Fangs," Pola said.

Darek's breath caught in his throat. "What?" he whispered hoarsely.

"Didn't they tell you?" Pola asked quietly. "That's what they raise them for."

7

Darek and Pola sat staring at the empty table in front of them. Darek's stomach was hollow and aching, and his blistered hands stung. He and Pola hadn't finished their chores fast enough to suit Daxon.

"I'm sorry I wasn't faster," Darek said. "This is my fault."

Pola waved his words away. "I didn't finish in time my first day, either," he said. "You'll be faster tomorrow."

And Darek would, he vowed, if it killed him.

Pola would not have to go hungry another day on his account.

"Wench! More slog!" Daxon yelled from a nearby table.

A young girl, around Darek's age, made her way among the tables. She was balancing a heavy tray of foaming mugs.

"Faster!" Daxon bellowed.

"I'm moving as fast as I can!" the girl snapped. She reached Daxon and banged a mug down in front of him. Flecks of foam splashed up into his face. Daxon grabbed her wrist and glared into her eyes. She glared back. Darek held his breath, wondering what would happen next.

Daxon began to laugh. "Spirit!" he said, releasing her wrist. "I like a wench with spirit. Too bad you Zorians are so ugly."

The girl whirled and stomped away, and Daxon and his friends had another laugh.

Ugly? Darek thought. He saw nothing ugly about the girl. He thought her quite beautiful, in fact. And he also admired her spirit.

"What is a Zorian?" he asked Pola.

"We are Zorians," Pola said. "At least, that's what the Kradens call us."

"Are all . . ."

"No more questions." Pola put a finger to his lips and nodded toward Daxon, who was eyeing them suspiciously. "We are forbidden to speak of anything but our work."

Darek's tiny cell of a room was cold and dark. The walls were rough gray stone, and there was one small barred window. He shivered as he lay on his pallet, a threadbare blanket clutched tightly around him. His body was exhausted, but his mind was even more tired. All day, he'd been straining to remember who he was, where he had come from. But the effort had given him nothing more than a pounding headache.

Darek's thoughts were suddenly interrupted by a soft scraping noise. He sat up, clutching his blanket close.

One of the large stones in the wall near the floor was moving!

As Darek watched, the stone slid slowly into the room, and a face appeared. A body followed the face, and then another. Soon four boys and two girls had crawled into the room. Pola was among them, and so was the girl who had spilled slog on Daxon.

The boy who had been first to appear pressed a finger to his lips in warning. "I am Arnod," he whispered. "We come in friendship."

"What if they find you here?" Darek asked.

Arnod snorted softly. "They'll feed us all to the Red Fangs," he said.

Darek's eyes widened, but Arnod waved his worries away. "They won't find us," he said. "Daxon and his men drink themselves into a stupor every night. They have no knowledge of our meetings."

One of the girls smiled. "They think us simple-minded fools," she added. "It suits our purpose to let them believe that."

Darek nodded his understanding, and the slaves sat down cross-legged around his pallet. They told him their names, and the one named Arnod leaned forward.

"You and Rowena are new," Arnod said, nodding toward the girl who had spilled the slog. "And Pola arrived just last week. There must be a connection. What can you tell us of who you are or how you came here?"

Darek sighed and slowly shook his head. "I remember nothing," he whispered.

"Nor I," Rowena added.

The faces of Arnod and the others fell.

"I'm sorry," Darek said.

"It's all right," Arnod said. "It was the same with Pola. It has always been the same. We were hoping you might be from Zoriak. But we aren't even sure such a place exists anymore . . ."

"Zoriak?" Darek repeated. "What is Zoriak?"

Arnod sighed. "It is a long story. Our legends tell us that this valley was once called Zor. It was peaceful and beautiful then, and the mountains that ringed it were green and full of life. Only Zorians lived here."

"What happened?" Rowena asked.

"The Kradens came, from Beyond. They were bigger and stronger. They conquered most of us and made us slaves, but a few Zorians escaped over the mountains. In the Long Ago, some of them would come back and try to help us escape, too. They talked of a land they had named Zoriak, which means New Zor. They said we could live there in freedom. But few of those escapes succeeded, and then the mountains died. Those who came after that, like you, knew nothing of Zoriak."

"How did the mountains die?" Darek asked.

"The dragonsbreath," Arnod explained. "For some reason, it clings to the mountain peaks, killing everything."

"If the Red Fangs are the cause of the dragonsbreath," Rowena said, "why do the Kradens breed them?"

"They love blood sport," Arnod said. "They compete to raise the biggest and fiercest dragons. Then they pit them against one another and wager on the outcome. The Kradens use them in battle, too. King Zahr is at war with his brother Rebbe, whose kingdom lies south of the Great Plain of Krad."

Darek's eyes widened. "King Zahr makes war against his own brother?"

"Yes." Arnod nodded. "They had a falling-out long ago over a prize Red Fang. They have been at war ever since."

"This Zoriak," said Rowena. "Has anyone ever gone in search of it?"

Arnod shook his head. "No. The Kradens have no interest in the place. Besides, they cannot tolerate the dragonsbreath in the mountains. It is poison to them in such density. Zorians tolerate it better, but it addles their brains."

It was all too much. Darek's head was growing heavy from the talk. He was even starting to hear strange sounds, like dragon whimpers, in his ears. He caught Rowena's eye and saw that she looked as tired and confused as he.

Pola reached out and clapped them both on the arm. "Enough talk for one night, friends," he said. "We will speak of these things again soon. For now, you must sleep."

8

The next day, Darek worked at a furious pace. He refused to give in to his hunger or fatigue, refused to pay heed to his swollen hands or aching back. There would be dinner tonight, he was sure. He was keeping right up with Pola, despite the annoying little Blue. The dragonling still kept butting him playfully and darting in to give him quick licks on the cheek.

"Go away!" Darek shouted repeatedly. At times, he gave the little beast a gentle shove or raised his arm to block its advances.

"*Rrronk,*" the little creature would whimper. Darek had no intention of encouraging it in any way, though. He had enough to worry about without getting attached to a Red Fang's dinner.

"Persistent, isn't he?" Pola remarked.

"Yes." Darek frowned. "Why doesn't he bother you? Why is it just me?"

Pola shrugged. "He used to hang around me, until you arrived. But he was nowhere near as affectionate with me. It's almost like he knows you."

Darek felt a little prickle run up his spine. He stared at the dragon. "Maybe he does," he said softly. "Remember that pocket business yesterday?"

Pola paused in his work and gave Darek a long, thoughtful look. He glanced over his shoulders to see if Daxon or any of his men were around, then moved closer.

"It's curious," he said. "The other slaves say that the Blues arrived the same day I did. They've been wondering where they came from.

There haven't been any Blues here in the stock-yard for many years. The Kradens don't usually raise them, because they're so large and fierce. The Red Fangs have a hard time killing them."

A door opened, and Darek turned to see the girl, Rowena, come in with a broom. She walked by, sweeping.

"Thrummm!" Darek sang out. The next thing he knew, he was dancing around the girl, butting her with his head.

"What are you doing?" she cried. She whacked at him with her broom.

"Thrummm, thrummm," Darek sang. And then the little Blue was there, dancing and *thrumming,* too. Round and round the girl they both frolicked.

"Enough!" a voice boomed.

A whip lashed out and stung Darek a blow on the back. Stunned, he found himself hoisted up, dangling in front of Daxon's eyes.

"What kind of foolishness is this?" the Master roared.

Darek shook his head hard.

"Um . . . I . . . I don't know," he stammered. "Something came over me. I'm sorry."

"You'll be sorry, all right," the Master said, "when you don't eat again tonight! Pola, tether that dragon in the pen. Wench! Back to the kitchen with you!"

Darek looked at the sad little dragon as Pola led it away. For an instant, something seemed to pass between them. It was too fast-moving, too vague to capture, but it felt strangely like a memory.

Darek felt himself blushing when the slaves filed into his room that night. How could he explain his silly actions to Rowena?

"I'm sorry about today," he began.

"No need." Rowena gave him a strange look. "I understand."

"You do?"

She nodded. "I think so."

"Understand what?" Arnod asked.

Darek turned to him. "I think one of the Blue dragons might hold the key to who we are," he whispered. "I've got to find a way to spend more time with him."

"But how could a dragon help us?" Arnod asked.

"I don't know," Darek said. "I just think he can."

"Yes." Rowena nodded. "Darek's right. I feel it, too."

Arnod shrugged. "It won't be easy to arrange," he said. "And there may not be much time left."

"Time left?" Darek wrinkled his brow. "What do you mean?"

"The Kradens will probably feed him and the other Blues to the Fangs early, before they grow too big and strong."

"Then we have to start soon," Darek said. "Tonight, if possible."

Arnod sat back and chewed his lip thoughtfully. "We have passages all through the complex," he said. "But Daxon posts a watch on the nursery and stables at night. It would be too dangerous to go there."

"There must be somewhere else," Darek said.

"There's the granary, next to the nursery," Arnod said. "We may be able to sneak the Blue in there. It's dangerous, though. Very dangerous. If the creature makes a noise—if you are discovered—the passages, everything will be uncovered. We could all be fed to the Fangs."

Darek shivered, but then he took a deep breath and squared his shoulders. "You speak longingly of freedom," he said, "but you will never taste it unless you make it happen. And you cannot make it happen without taking risks. I, for one, would rather die than spend the rest of my life a slave." He looked around the circle of faces. "What about you?"

Pola leaned forward quickly and clapped a hand on Darek's knee. "I'm with you, my friend," he said.

Rowena nodded. "I, too."

Arnod and the others exchanged glances, then one by one they nodded as well. Arnod stretched his right arm out toward the center of the circle, and the others did the same. Darek placed his hand on top.

"To freedom!" he said.

9

"*Thrummm, thrummm, thrummm,*" the drag-onling sang softly.

Darek stroked its head and looked deep into its eyes. "Do you know me, young one?" he asked. "Have we been friends in another place?"

Warm feelings flowed into Darek's mind. Joy, love—emotions strangely out of place in this cold, dark granary. But that was all he seemed to get from the dragon—just feelings.

Though he was disappointed, Darek murmured gently and stroked the little beast's blue-scaled back. When his hand reached the wing bindings, he felt something sticky and wet. He pulled his hand away and looked at it.

Blood.

"Poor thing," he said. "Why didn't you let us know your bindings were cutting you? Here, let me help."

Carefully, Darek unwound the bindings until the little creature fluttered its wings.

"*Thrummm, thrummm,*" it cried again. In its joy, it fluttered right up off the floor.

"Shush," Darek said, laughing softly. Then, as he watched the beast flutter around the room, an idea slowly came to him. If he brought the dragonling here every night and let him exercise his wings, he might still be able to fly. And if he could fly, then somehow, someday, Darek might be able to ride him back to where he came from. Back to . . . "Home," Darek whispered, looking deeply into the dragon's eyes again. "Do you want to take me *home?*"

Suddenly, an image sprang into Darek's mind, an image that the dragonling seemed to be sending. It was a lovely farmhouse with rolling green pastures around it. There was a barn, too, filled with bales of sweet-smelling zorgrass. Outside, in the paddock, a boy was playing with a little Blue dragon. When the boy called out the beast's name, Darek's breath caught in his throat.

"Zantor," he whispered, still gazing into the dragon's eyes. "That's your name! And that's our home, yours and mine, isn't it?"

The little forked tongue flicked out and planted a kiss on his cheek. *"Thrummm,"* Zantor sang. *"Thrummm, thrummm, thrummm."*

Darek smiled and rubbed the nubby head. "Pola," he said. "Tell me about Pola."

Images filled Darek's head again, pictures of Darek, Zantor, and Pola. First they were romping through fields, then splashing in a brook. Lastly he saw the three of them lazing in front of a crackling fire.

"So, he's my best friend," Darek said. "No wonder I like him so well. And what of the girl, Rowena?"

Warm, loving feelings flooded through Darek. He felt the touch of gentle hands and saw beautiful eyes staring into his. For a moment, he could hardly breathe. Then he laughed softly.

"She's very special to you, isn't she, Zantor?" he whispered.

"*Thrummm,*" Zantor sang.

The long days of toil passed quickly for Darek. He worked harder than any of the other slaves, and muscles began to bulge on his back and arms. Whenever Daxon sent for him or assigned him a new task, he went out of his way to please. He wanted Daxon to be happy, to enjoy every drop of his evening slog, and to stay far away from the granary at night.

Darek and his friends had begun training Zantor and some of the other dragons to fly with riders on their backs. Little by little, Zantor was giving Darek and Rowena and Pola their memories back. They, in turn, shared what they learned with the others. There were still many gaps, but this much they knew: Zoriak *was* real, a beautiful green place, with sparkling clear air. Freedom waited there, and their families, too, if only they could figure out how to return. Exactly where Zoriak was, they still didn't know. But Darek was confident that Zantor would be able to remember and lead them there.

Darek, Pola, Rowena, Arnod, and the others had fashioned saddles and bridles out of bits of cloth and leather. Working together each night, they soon became friends. The dragons were growing bigger every day. Before long, they would all make their escape.

There was still the dragonsbreath to contend with, of course. But Darek, Pola, and Rowena knew they had come through it once without losing their wits, so there had to be a chance of doing it again. It was only a chance, of course, but it was a chance they were willing to take.

10

Darek had been assigned to the stalls instead of the nursery all morning. At lunchtime, he looked up to see Pola running toward him. He was pale and out of breath.

"What is it?" Darek asked. "What's wrong?"

Pola looked around nervously. "The Blues!" he whispered. "They took one of them early this morning!"

"What?" Darek felt the blood draining from his face. "Which one?"

"Leezin, the one Arnod was training.

She's . . . she's dead by now, fed to the Red Fangs."

Tears sprang to Darek's eyes. Gentle Leezin—dead?

"They could take the others as soon as tomorrow!" Pola warned.

Darek stared down at the floor, and his feet blurred through his tears. Zantor—fed to the Red Fangs tomorrow! He could not bear to think of it. Then he realized something else. Everything they had worked for, everything they had planned, would all be gone without the dragons. He sucked in a deep breath and looked up again.

"We must leave tonight," he said.

Pola's eyes widened. "Tonight! But the dragons aren't strong enough," he said. "We'll never make it."

"Then we'll die trying," Darek said.

It was decided that only Darek, Pola, and Rowena would go. Their Blues were bigger and

stronger than the other dragons and stood a chance of success. Trying to fly the smaller dragons while they were still so young would have been much too dangerous for riders and dragons alike.

Well after dark, Darek, Pola, and Rowena stood in a circle in the granary with the others. They reached their hands into the center.

"We will be back, my friends," Darek said.

"We will be waiting," Arnod replied.

"Train as many dragons as you can," Darek said. "They will be useful when the time comes."

Arnod and the others nodded.

Darek felt tears start behind his eyes. He and his friends were being brave, but in their hearts they knew they might never see one another again. It would be a miracle if the escape succeeded, and, whatever the result, it would surely bring the wrath of Zahr down on those who remained behind. But it did no good to dwell on such things. They had no choice.

"The alarms will sound as soon as the doors open," Arnod warned. "Your only hope will be to get a strong head start before they get the Fangs into the air."

"We will," Darek assured him. He mounted Zantor, and Pola and Rowena mounted the two remaining Blues.

"Now!" he commanded Arnod.

Arnod and the others pulled back the granary doors. Immediately, the piercing shriek of a siren split the air. Darek shouted the flight command, and the three dragons pushed off with their powerful legs, pumping their small wings mightily. The ground began to fall away beneath them.

"We're going to make it!" Pola shouted.

"Yes!" Rowena cried out. "We're going home!"

Darek wasn't quite as certain. He could feel Zantor's heart pounding against his knees. He and the others were heavy burdens for dragons so young. Below them, Krad was springing to

life. Men scurried everywhere. Arrows were shot into the air but fell far short of their mark. Before long, though, Darek heard the horrible screams of Red Fangs. He looked back and saw several beasts and riders in pursuit.

"Home, Zantor, home!" he cried. "Faster!"

Zantor pumped his wings harder, but arrows whizzed around them now. The Red Fangs were fast approaching. Soon they would be within flaming distance. Darek glanced from left to right. Pola and Rowena were still with him, and the mountains were drawing closer. If they could just make it into the thick of the mist, they would be safe. The Kradens could not pursue them there. But Zantor's heart was thumping rapidly now. How much longer could he endure?

Suddenly, there was a burst of flame off to Darek's right. A Red Fang was gaining on him. The flame came again, closer. Darek cried out and dropped the reins as his sleeve caught fire.

"You okay?" Pola called.

"Yes!" Darek lurched wildly, trying to beat out the flames. He gripped Zantor's back with just his knees. Rowena flew in close and tried desperately to help him. The mist was thickening. Safety was so close!

"Go on!" Darek called to Rowena as he tried to shrug out of his burning shirt. "Whatever happens, just keep going!"

Then there was a searing pain in his leg. Darek stared mutely at the arrow shaft and the widening circle of red. Another arrow whizzed by, plunging into Zantor's neck. *"Eeeiiieee!"* Zantor screamed. And then they were falling . . .

11

"Well, well. Good morning."

Darek blinked to clear the haze from his eyes. A great fur-covered face stared down at him—a Kraden. He swallowed hard as the truth sank in. He had been captured again. He tried to move but winced in pain. Where was he? he wondered. He blinked again and looked around. He appeared to be in a cave of some sort, lit by torches on the walls.

"Who are you?" he asked the Kraden. "Where am I?"

"I am Azzon," the man said, "the rightful King of Krad. You are in my chambers. The Zynots brought you here."

"Zynots?" Darek mumbled.

"The little creatures who inhabit these mountains," the man explained. "They tell me you did them a kindness in the past. They wished to repay it."

Azzon nodded at Darek's leg. Darek looked down and saw that it had been wrapped in a plaster and bandaged.

"I have no memory of Zynots," he said. "Nor do I think it a kindness to deliver me back into Kraden hands."

"We are not in Kraden hands," a voice said. "Azzon is a friend."

Darek turned to see Rowena ducking through a low door. Pola followed her into the room.

"What are you two doing here?" Darek cried.

"We came back when you fell," Pola said.

"You fools!" Darek shook his head. "I told you to keep going!"

"It is well that they did not," Azzon said, "or they would be witless by now."

"We've already been through the mountains once," Darek argued. "The dragonsbreath did not harm us."

"Your lungs were clean and strong then," Azzon said. "You have lived too long in Krad now. You would not have made it this time."

Darek turned back to Pola and Rowena. "Zantor?" he asked. "What of Zantor?

Pola and Rowena exchanged troubled glances. "We don't know," Pola said quietly. "He disappeared after you fell."

Darek was silent, remembering the arrow.

"We freed our dragons," Rowena said, "and sent them after him. They'll find him."

Darek bit his lip, close to tears. Poor Zantor. Even if the other dragons did find him, how could they help if he was hurt or dying?

12

Azzon sat back in his chair and puffed slowly on a long clay pipe.

"There is not much more to tell," he said. "Kradens have always known of the existence of Zoriak, but it never troubled us. The few Zorians who came over the mountains were easily dealt with. The dragonsbreath potion quickly robbed them of their memories. In time, our Zorian slaves began to wonder if the old legends of Zoriak were even true."

"What about the Zynots?" Darek asked. "Who are they?"

Azzon laughed. "Your ancient kin," he said. "They are Zorians who lost their wits and their way in the Long Ago. In time, their bodies changed. Now they are prisoners of the mountain, able to breathe only dragonsbreath." Azzon pulled thoughtfully at the graying fur on his chin. "They are timid and foolish," he said, "but kind and good, too. I owe my life to them."

"Your life?" Rowena's brow wrinkled in disbelief. "How came the King of Krad to owe his life to Zynots?"

Azzon smiled sadly. "As you have seen," he said, "Kradens love blood sport, and I, their king, loved it better than any other. There was never a dragon fight bloody enough for me, a battle fierce enough, until the day my sons Zahr and Rebbe turned on each other. It was then, and only then, that I saw what I had done to them. I had raised them like Red Fangs, living

78

to kill. When I tried to stop them from killing each other, they turned their fury on me."

Azzon took a long puff on his pipe and stared blankly at the walls. Darek swallowed hard and glanced at Pola and Rowena.

"I fled into these mountains, expecting to die," Azzon went on softly. "The Zynots found me and brought me here, to this cave beneath the mountains. The dragonsbreath cannot penetrate here. The Zynots have seen to my needs ever since, but it is a lonely life. They cannot tarry long in my world, nor I in theirs."

"Is there no way out?" Darek asked.

"Not for me," Azzon said. Then he leaned forward and rested his arms on his knees. "But perhaps for you. Before we speak of it, though, you must explain something to me."

"What is that?" Darek asked.

Azzon narrowed his eyes. "How did you get your memories back?"

Darek straightened in his seat. He dared not tell Azzon the truth. Who knew if Azzon could be trusted? He scrambled to come up with an answer that would satisfy Azzon without giving away the secret of Zantor's mind messages. What was it Azzon had said earlier? Something about a dragonsbreath potion?

"We didn't get our memories back," Darek said quickly. "I . . . never really lost mine. I never drank the potion."

Azzon regarded him intently. "How can that be?"

Darek scrambled to think. His first memories of Krad were of a dark house, an old crone, and a guard. "The old woman gave me the potion," he explained, "but her house was dark and steamy. I tilted my head back and let it run out of the side of my mouth and down my neck. Then I pretended my memory was gone."

Azzon continued to stare hard at Darek. "How did you know the potion was meant to rob your memory?" he asked.

"The guard, Org, spoke of it."

After a time, Azzon nodded slowly. Then he

rose and reached for a shelf on the wall. He took down a vial of green liquid and three small cups. Then he turned to face Darek and the others again.

"Be assured," he said. "*I* will not be as careless as Jazee."

13

"But wait!" Darek jumped up. "You said you were a friend! Why are you sending us back?"

"I'm not sending you back," Azzon said. "I'm sending you home."

"Home?" Darek sat down again with a thump.

"Home?" Pola and Rowena echoed.

"Yes." Azzon nodded. "There is a tunnel. An underground passage to Zoriak. I will take you there tonight. But you must go without your memories."

"But our friends . . ." Pola started to protest.

"I cannot allow you to remember your friends," Azzon said. "You might try to help them."

"What's wrong with that?" Rowena asked. "Maybe we could help you, too."

Azzon shook his head. "If I wanted to help myself, I could go with you tonight," he said. "But I am old and wise. I know that things are not always as simple as they seem. Your world and mine are not ready to come together."

"Why not?" Darek asked. "Maybe we could make your world better."

"Better how?" Azzon asked. "By trying to destroy my sons? They may be cruel and evil, but they are still my sons. And what of the dragons of Krad, the mighty Red Fangs? Would you kill them? Then you might as well kill the Zynots, for they will die anyway without the dragons-breath. Have you the stomach for so much killing?"

Darek swallowed. He had no stomach for killing at all.

"Azzon is right," Rowena said sadly.

Pola nodded.

"But what of our friends?" Darek asked.

"If freedom means as much to your friends as it does to you," Azzon said, "they will find their own way."

14

Darek, Rowena, and Pola stood facing Azzon. The night air was soft and fragrant. Zoriak's twin moons smiled down on them, welcoming them home. Azzon took out his vial.

"Drink," he commanded, pouring them each a portion of the green liquid. "I have added something to make you sleep. When you wake in the morning, you will know your names and you will remember each other. But you will recall nothing that has happened for at least two or three anums . . ."

"Two or three anums!" Darek cried. "But . . . we won't even remember Zantor!"

"I'm sorry," Azzon said. "I cannot take the risk of allowing you to remember more. You must trust me. It is better this way." Then he smiled sadly and added, "Good life to you, my friends."

Darek, Pola, and Rowena slowly lifted their cups. "And to you, Azzon," they said softly. Then they tilted their heads and drank. Darek thought one last time about Arnod and the others.

"Farewell, my friends," he whispered. "Lord Eternal be with you." Then he thought about Zantor, and tears stung his eyes. "And with you, little friend," he whispered, "wherever you are."

Darek opened his eyes and blinked. He was in a gently sloping field of zorgrass.

"What?" he whispered. "What am I doing here?" He rolled over and blinked again. "Pola? Rowena?" he said. "What are we all doing here?"

Pola and Rowena sat up and looked around.

"We're in the foothills of the Yellow Mountains!" Pola said.

"How did we get *here?*" Rowena asked.

"I don't know." Darek shook his head. "I do know one thing, though. Our parents are going to kill us."

"Uh-oh." Rowena pointed up at the sky. "You mean, if *they* don't kill us first!"

Three young Blue dragons were winging their way over the Yellow Mountains.

"Stay calm," Darek said. "Maybe they won't see us."

"They see us, all right!" Pola shouted. "Here they come!"

They all jumped to their feet, and Rowena and Pola started to run. But for some reason, Darek didn't. Instead, he stood and watched the dragons dip lower, lower, until they landed right in front of him.

One of them, a male, stared at him with pain-filled eyes. *"Rrronk!"* he cried.

"Why, you're hurt!" Darek said. A broken arrow shaft protruded from the dragon's neck.

Darek approached carefully.

"Here," he said, grabbing the shaft. "Let me help." He pulled, and the arrow came out clean. The young dragon seemed tired but grateful. He laid his head gently on Darek's shoulder.

"Thrummm," he sang softly. *"Thrummm, thrummm, thrummm."*

"Why . . . they're friendly!" Rowena cried out.

Darek turned to see her and Pola watching in amazement.

"Is that one all right?" Pola asked, approaching cautiously.

"I think so." Darek reached up and gently stroked the dragon's neck. "Poor thing. I wonder who shot him? This arrow isn't Zorian."

The little dragon pulled back. He tilted his head and looked deeply into Darek's eyes. For an instant, something seemed to pass between them, something too fast-moving, too vague to capture.

Something that felt strangely like a memory.

Dragon Trouble

Prologue

Legend has it that the people of Zoriac originally came from a green valley called Zor, beyond the dreaded Black Mountains, and that fierce men known as Kradens drove them out and renamed the valley Krad. Some Zorians believe the legends. Others say that Zor was a mythical place and the great, hairy-faced Kradens are nothing but fairy tale creatures. No one knows for sure, because no one has ever ventured into the Black Mountains and returned to tell of it, until now.

When a runaway wagon carried Darek's best

friend, Pola, and four baby Blue dragons into the Black Mountains, Darek and Rowena, daughter of the Chief Elder, felt responsible. It was their selfishness that had led to the accident. Together, they defied the laws of Zoriac and went after their friends. Now the three children are back safely and they have rescued three of the four Blue dragons, including Darek's beloved dragon, Zantor. But all is not well. It seems that their fathers and Darek's brother, Clep, went into the mountains after them, and have not returned. The children are desperate to get their loved ones back, but they can't even remember how *they* got back. Their memories were erased in Krad. Zantor, who can send mind messages to Darek and Rowena, is helping them piece the past together, but it is slow going. Will they remember in time to save their fathers? Or is it already too late?

1

Darek sat on the paddock fence, staring. Out in the fields Zantor and the two female dragons, Drizba and Typra, grazed peacefully. The zorgrass obviously agreed with them. They had grown tremendously in the few weeks since Darek had been back at home. Zantor still insisted on sleeping by Darek's bed each night. But that couldn't go on much longer. Zantor could barely squeeze through the door anymore!

Little by little, Darek was trying to piece together what had happened to him since Zantor

came into his life. He and his friends Pola and
Rowena had been to Krad and back. He knew
that much. But someone, or something, had taken
away their memories while they were there. Not

just their memories of Krad, but their memories of several anums before, too. Darek's mother had been doing her best to fill in those anums for him.

Zantor was helping, too. He was able to send Darek and his friend Rowena mind pictures of things he had heard and seen. These mind messages were giving them back memories of Krad. Darek hadn't shared these memories with his mother yet because he didn't want to worry her. They were too awful to share—scenes of a bleak, smoke-shrouded land, where Zorians were slaves, and fierce, hairy Kradens ruled. Darek swallowed hard. His father and brother were still in Krad somewhere, and Pola's and Rowena's fathers, too. That is—if any of them were still alive.

Darek heard a shout and turned to see Pola and Rowena coming up the road.

"How's he doing?" asked Rowena. She hopped up on the fence and nodded toward the scar on Zantor's neck. Zantor and Darek had both been wounded by arrows in their escape from Krad.

"Good as new," said Darek. "Look at him."

The three friends watched as Zantor charged the other two dragons in a play battle. Drizba and Typra reared and screamed in mock terror. Darek, Pola, and Rowena laughed.

"How about you?" Pola asked then. "How's the leg coming along?"

Darek rubbed his thigh. "A little stiff still, but nothing I can't handle. Any further word on our punishment?"

"No." Rowena bit her lip. There was a law in Zoriac that anyone caught venturing into the Black Mountains was to be put to death. Pola did not need to worry. He had been carried into the mountains by accident. But Darek and Rowena had gone after him willingly. Under Zorian law, when a child under twelve broke the law, the child's father was made to suffer the punishment, even if that father was Chief Elder, like Rowena's father. But Darek's father and the Chief Elder were gone, along with Pola's father and Darek's brother. They had gone into the Black Mountains, too, to search for the children. And they had not returned.

"It's all so confusing," Rowena went on. "Mother says the elders can't decide what to do. I worry what will happen when our fathers get back, though. Zarnak, the acting chief, seems very fond of that crown on his head. I think he will be all too glad of a reason to put my father to death."

Pola shook his head firmly. "Your father has too many friends on the Council," he said to Rowena. "And Darek, your father is one of the most respected men in the village. Don't worry about that old law. It was only made to scare Zorians away from the Black Mountains for their own safety."

"That's not quite true," said Rowena. "It was also meant to prevent Zorians from going over the mountains and provoking the Kradens, *if* they in fact existed."

"*Thrummm, thrummm, thrummm!*" The young dragons had noticed the children and came loping over. They stuck their heads over the fence to be petted.

"Here," Darek said, pulling some sugar cubes from his jerkin pocket. He handed a few to Pola and Rowena. "Zantor reminded me yesterday that he loves these."

The three children held out the cubes and, *thwippp, thwippp, thwippp!* The dragons gobbled them eagerly.

"Have you gotten any more mind messages from Zantor?" Rowena asked Darek as they watched the dragons munch.

"Shush!" Darek glanced back toward the house. "I don't think my mother, or anyone else, should know what we've found out about Krad until we can figure a way to get our fathers back."

"Why?" asked Rowena.

"Because I don't trust Zarnak. As far as I'm concerned, the less he knows, the better."

Rowena and Pola nodded their agreement.

"The last memory I can get from Zantor," Darek went on, "is when the arrow struck my leg.

But . . . how did we get home? We made it through the mists *somehow*."

Pola and Rowena nodded again. They had learned from Zantor's mind messages that the mists in the Black Mountains were poisonous. The poison was deadly to Kradens, and robbed Zorians of their minds.

"We've *got* to find out how we did it," said Darek.

"Why?" asked Pola. "What are you planning?"

Darek glanced toward the house and then lowered his voice. "I'm going back," he said.

A wry smile slowly curled Pola's lips. "When do we leave?" he asked.

"I didn't say *we*," said Darek. "I said *me*. I'm already in trouble. You're not."

Pola bristled. "Oh, right," he said, "like I'd ever let you go alone. My father's over there, too, don't forget."

"And mine!" Rowena put in.

Both boys turned to look at her. "You're not

suggesting we take *you* back there?" said Darek. "It's too dangerous!"

Rowena crossed her arms over her chest and narrowed her eyes. "Nobody *takes* me anywhere," she said. "I go where I *please*. And *if* I please to go with you, I *will*. Just like I did last time."

"*Rrronk!*" came a sudden cry. The young dragons had finished the sugar cubes and gone back to their games. Apparently Zantor had started playing a little too rough, knocking Drizba down. As Darek, Pola, and Rowena watched, Drizba got to her feet, threw back her head, and spread her wings.

"*Grrrawwk!*" she screamed in a *very* convincing imitation of an angry, full-grown Blue.

"*Rrronk, rrronk!*" cried Zantor. He barreled across the field, leapt the fence in a single bound, and dove for cover behind Darek.

"Wow," said Darek, "she's pretty impressive when she gets mad. I thought for a minute she was going to breathe fire."

"Who?" asked Pola, grinning widely, "Drizba, or Rowena?"

2

"Mother?" Darek called.

"Up here," Alayah answered.

Darek climbed the narrow, winding staircase to the garret.

"Rrronk," cried Zantor. Darek looked back and saw him wedged in the doorway. The garret stairs were too narrow for him.

"Silly dragon," said Darek. He went back down and pushed Zantor free. "Just wait here," he said. "I'll only be a moment." Zantor's head sagged. He rested his chin on one of the lower steps and watched sadly as Darek climbed up, out of his reach.

Alayah was just closing an old chest as Darek entered the garret. She dabbed quickly at her eyes with her apron.

"What are you doing?" Darek asked.

"Nothing," she said, "just . . ." Her voice trailed off.

Darek walked over and crouched down beside her. "What's in here?" he asked. Before his mother could answer, he lifted the lid and looked in. The chest was full of yellowed letters and baby clothes. Some of his father's old uniforms, medals, and archery trophies were there, too.

"Just memories," Darek's mother said softly.

Darek lifted out one of the trophies and sat with it on his lap. He thought of the days when he and Clep were small. Often, in the evenings, after supper, his father would set a target up beyond the barn and let them practice with his great bow. At first Darek had been too small even to bend the string, but his father would twine his fingers through Darek's and help him pull.

"You did it!" Clep would cry when the arrow found its mark. Then Darek would feel proud, even though he knew he couldn't have done it without his father.

Tears sprang to Darek's eyes. How he missed his father and brother. Sadly, he replaced the trophy in the chest. He was about to close it again when he noticed something in the corner. It looked like a mask of some sort.

"What's this?" he asked, lifting the object out.

"Oh, that old thing," his mother said, wrinkling her nose. "That was your great-grandfather's battle mask."

"Battle mask?" Darek repeated. "I never heard of a battle mask."

"The men haven't used them since the Red Fangs disappeared," Alayah explained.

Darek's ears perked up. There were still Red Fangs in Krad—hundreds of them! It was their breath that poisoned the mists in the mountains.

"Why did the men wear masks to fight the Red Fangs?" he asked.

"Something about their breath," his mother replied. "It was poisonous, I think."

Darek's heart thumped quickly as he turned the strange mask over in his hand. "And the masks filtered the poison out?" he asked.

"I believe so." His mother nodded.

Darek couldn't believe his ears. This was it! This was his answer! Now he could go back to Krad.

"Are there any more of these?" he asked.

"A few perhaps, in the archives in Elder Hall. Why?"

When Darek didn't answer right away a cloud of fear darkened Alayah's eyes. Her hand went to her chest.

"What are you thinking?" she asked worriedly.

Darek looked at her. He couldn't lie to her— couldn't leave her again without explanation.

"These masks make it possible for me to go after Father and Clep," he said.

A small cry escaped Alayah's lips and tears filled her eyes again. "Oh, I was afraid of this," she said softly.

"I must go," Darek said gently. "Please . . . don't try to stop me."

His mother wiped her tears and put her arms around him. "I would try, if I could," she said with a sigh, "but I know I can't. Trying to stop you from following your heart is like trying to stop a river from flowing. You'll only boil and churn until you find another way to burst out and rush away."

Darek looked up into his mother's eyes. He'd never known she was so wise, and brave. "Thank you for understanding," he said.

"Thank *you* for giving me a chance to say good-bye this time," she answered.

3

Darek, Pola, and Rowena crouched in the bushes below Elder Hall. The building was tall and imposing. Fierce stone dragon heads glared down at them from the rooftop. A pair of armed guards flanked the door.

"How are we supposed to get past them?" Darek whispered.

"Maybe there's another way in," said Pola.

Rowena shook her head. "The back door is kept chained and barred," she said. "There's only one way in and you're looking at it."

"Then we need a decoy," said Darek. He looked at Rowena.

She frowned. "Why me?" she asked. "Why can't one of you be the decoy?"

"Because they all know you," said Darek. "Your father's Chief Elder."

"Which is why Zarnak hates me," Rowena reminded him. "He'd love another chance to humiliate me and my family."

"But the guards are still loyal to your father," said Darek. "They'll help you. You know they will."

Rowena looked at Darek doubtfully. "What do you want me to do?" she asked.

"I don't know. Pretend you're hurt or something."

Rowena huffed. "I don't like it," she said. "Why do I have to be the damsel in distress while you get to have all the fun?"

Darek snorted. "Fun?" he said. "Sneaking around in the dungeons of that creepy old hall? I'd be happy to trade places, but be serious. If

Pola or I go up there and fall on our faces in front of those guys they'll just laugh their heads off."

Rowena rolled her eyes. "All right, I'll do it," she said. "But I won't like it."

"Nobody's asking you to like it," said Darek. "Just get going, okay? Time's wasting."

Rowena slipped around to the side of the building and back down the hillside. Darek and Pola crept farther up the bank. They waited, hidden, just below the front steps.

"Lady Rowena!" they heard one of the guards shout after a while.

"Good morning," they heard Rowena call from below. Then a cry. "Aaagh!"

Darek winked at Pola. "Very convincing," he whispered.

"Milady!" both guards cried at once. They dropped their lances and hurried down the stairs.

Darek and Pola crept out of the bushes and up the steps, keeping deep in the shadows.

"Oww, oww, oooh," they heard Rowena moan.

They could see her writhing on the ground with both guards bent over her.

"Hurry," said Darek as he pushed one of the great doors open. Both boys slipped inside, scurried for a dark corner, and stopped to catch their breath.

There was no one in sight. They listened for voices or footsteps, but there were none. Elder Hall was silent and forbidding, lit only by flickering torchlight. Darek and Pola stared in awe. Neither had ever been inside before. They were in a small entry hall. An arched doorway beyond led into the Council Room. Darek and Pola crept forward to have a better look.

"Wow," whispered Darek. Adorning the walls were dragon skins of all colors. They hung at angles as if diving out of the sky. Their tails curled up and across the great, high ceiling. Their glassy eyes were fixed on the Council Table, which stretched the length of the room. Their mouths gaped open, fangs barred, in imitation of battle screams. On an elevated platform at the far end of the room stood the Chief Elder's throne. It was carved in the shape of a sitting dragon. The head was real—it was the stuffed head of a Great Blue.

Darek shuddered. "I'm glad we didn't bring Zantor," he said.

Pola nodded. "Yeah. Let's get this over with. This place gives me the creeps."

Darek looked around. To one side of the front doors a stairway wound down into darkness.

"Grab a torch and follow me," he said.

He and Pola grabbed the two closest torches and started down. The stairs grew steeper and narrower as they went. At the bottom was a long, narrow passageway with doors opening off each side.

"Where do we start?" asked Pola. "We don't have much time. Those guards aren't going to listen to Rowena whine forever."

Darek pushed a door open and thrust his torch inside. "Lord E . . . !" he cried.

"What is it?" asked Pola, trying to peek around him.

"I think it's an old torture chamber of some kind," Darek whispered. "Look."

He stood to one side and Pola peeked in. The room was so thick with cobwebs it was hard to see. There were spikes sticking everywhere out of the walls and up from the floor. Chains dangled from ceiling and walls.

"Lord Eternal," whispered Pola. "There's no place to sit or lie down without being pierced!"

"And we thought the Kradens were cruel," said Darek. "Looks like Zorians can be pretty cruel, too."

Suddenly there was a sound overhead. It sounded like footsteps. Darek and Pola froze. A minute went by, then two. The sound didn't come again.

"Our imaginations must be playing tricks on us," said Darek. "Come on. Let's find those masks and get out of here."

They peeked into a number of other chambers and cells, until at last they came to a room filled with dusty trunks and cupboards.

"This looks like the archives," Darek whispered. "Hurry."

They put their torches into holders on the walls and started tearing open drawers and throwing back the lids of trunks. They found stacks of old books and scrolls, chests full of rusted armor and old weapons.

"Here they are!" Pola cried at last.

Darek ran over and looked down. In the chest at Pola's feet lay a mound of battle masks.

"Great!" cried Darek. He grabbed several of the masks and shoved them inside his shirt. Pola did the same.

"That should do it," said Darek. "Let's go."

They turned toward the door, but then froze in their tracks. Leaning against the door frame, arms folded over his chest, was Zarnak!

"Interested in history, are you, boys?" he asked wryly.

4

Darek, Pola, and Rowena waited off to one side. Their mothers stood before Zarnak. The battle masks lay in a heap on the Council table.

"Why were your children in the archives?" Zarnak demanded. "What use have they for these masks?"

Rowena's mother, the Grand Dame, shrugged. "They are children," she said.

"Yes," Pola's mother chimed in. "You know how curious children are. I'll wager you tried to sneak into Elder Hall yourself as a boy."

Zarnak did not look amused. He turned toward Darek and Pola.

"What use have you for these masks?" he repeated.

"We were going play Dragon Quest with them," said Darek.

"Yes," agreed Pola. "It was just a game."

Zarnak's eyes narrowed.

"A game, eh?" he said. "A game like . . . trying to rescue your fathers?"

Darek's heart thumped. "N-no," he stammered.

"Would that they *could* rescue their fathers," the Grand Dame interrupted angrily. "But look at them. They are but children. It is you, Zarnak, who should be about the business of rescuing their fathers."

Zarnak shifted uncomfortably in his seat. "You know the Council voted against a rescue," he said. "We still don't know what dangers lie beyond the Black Mountains. If these children had not disobeyed the law in the first place their fathers would not be in trouble. Your husband, Grand

Dame, would not wish me to place the whole village at risk for his sake."

The Grand Dame's eyes flashed. "You may fool others with that lie, Zarnak," she said. "But you don't fool me. I know who swayed the Council against a rescue, and I can well see how fond you've grown of that throne."

Zarnak and the Grand Dame stared at each other in stony silence for a long moment, then he motioned to the guards. "Escort these women and children to the door!" he shouted.

As Pola, Rowena, and Darek turned to go, Zarnak pointed a sharp finger at them. "Be warned," he boomed. "Children or not, I will have you in the stocks the next time I catch you sneaking about!"

5

After supper, Darek's mother went out on an errand. Darek, Pola, and Rowena sat beside the hearth. Zantor, who now filled half the room, sprawled behind them, with his neck over Darek's shoulder and his head in Rowena's lap.

"We've *got* to find a way to go back," said Rowena. She looked down into Zantor's eyes. "Tell us more, Zantor," she said. "We must know how we got out of Krad."

Darek reached up on the mantel and took down the arrow that he had pulled from Zantor's neck.

He placed the point over the wound in his leg and made a motion like he was pulling it out. "Who took the arrow out of my leg, Zantor?" he asked. "Do you remember anything?"

The young dragon stared at the arrow. A misty image began to take shape in Darek's mind. "I'm getting something!" said Rowena.

"Shush!" said Darek. "Me, too." In his head he saw his own body lying crumpled on the rocky soil of the Black Mountains. Bent little creatures crowded around him. One of them grasped the arrow shaft and pulled it free. Then the image started to fade.

"What else, Zantor?" asked Darek. "Who are those creatures? Where did they take me?"

But Zantor's great, green eyes only stared at him blankly.

"What did he show you?" asked Pola.

"The creatures who rescued me," said Darek. "But I have no idea who or what they are."

"If only we could find them," said Rowena. "If

they helped us, maybe they helped our fathers and Clep, too."

"Not much chance of finding them without the masks," said Darek quietly.

Suddenly the door opened and Darek's mother rushed in. With her was the Grand Dame herself.

"Mother!" cried Rowena in surprise. She, Darek, and Pola jumped to their feet.

"Hurry," whispered the Grand Dame, motioning to someone still outside. A guard entered, bearing a chest.

"What the . . . ?" said Darek.

"Put them there," the Grand Dame commanded, pointing to the kitchen table. "Then be gone. You have seen nothing and heard nothing. Do you understand?"

The guard nodded. He lowered the chest to the table, and emptied its contents.

"The masks!" cried Darek.

The guard slipped silently back out into the night. The Grand Dame closed the door after him. Then she turned and smiled.

"My husband has many friends," she said. Then she looked at Rowena. "Why did you not seek my help at the outset?" she asked.

"I . . . I did not think you would be willing," said Rowena.

The Grand Dame came forward and gently smoothed her daughter's hair. She put a hand on Rowena's shoulder and gazed proudly but sadly into her eyes. "Did you think," she said gently, "that Alayah was the only mother capable of understanding the destiny of her child?"

Zantor, Drizba, and Typra were saddled and ready to go. The young dragons were in high spirits. They seemed eager for the adventure, but Darek, Pola, and Rowena were solemn. Their mothers stood beside them in the early morning chill.

"Is it cold in Krad?" Darek's mother asked. "Perhaps you should bring cloaks."

"Yes, and rain hoods," said the Grand Dame. "Wait a bit. I'll run back and get them." She turned and took a step but Rowena called her back. Rowena, Pola, and Darek exchanged glances. They knew their mothers were raising these small worries to keep from voicing the larger ones. And to forestall the leavetaking.

"We have to go," Darek told the women quietly. "The longer we wait, the greater the chance the elders will discover us."

The three mothers nodded bravely, but all of them blinked back tears.

"Take care," Alayah whispered. She stepped forward and kissed Darek good-bye. Then she patted Zantor's neck. "Watch over him, my friend," she pleaded softly. Zantor tossed his head regally as if to say, "Fear not."

Darek climbed into the saddle and fitted his mask over his face. "Ready?" he called to Pola and Rowena. His voice, through the mask, had a muffled, metallic sound.

Pola and Rowena kissed their mothers good-bye, then mounted their dragons and put on their masks. In their saddlebags were the remaining masks. There were just enough for the fathers and Clep, and one spare. The others had been too old and rotted to be of use.

"Ready," Pola and Rowena cried.

"Push off!" Darek commanded.

Zantor crouched down, unfurled his wings, and then sprang upward! With a mighty downward

sweep of wings, they were airborne. Darek felt a rush of exhilaration.

"We'll be back!" he cried over his shoulder. Their mothers, waving below, grew smaller as the ground fell away. "And Clep and our fathers will be with us!" Darek promised.

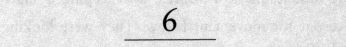

6

Thick, damp smoke swirled around them. But thanks to the masks, Darek, Pola, and Rowena could not smell the foul breath of the Black Mountains. Below them the landscape was barren and forbidding. There were rocks and stumps and scrubby bushes. Everything was black and charred, as if it had been swept by a forest fire.

Zantor seemed to know where he was going. He and the other dragons were flying strongly. They seemed to have no problem carrying riders anymore.

"Stay close," Darek called to Pola and Rowena as the smog thickened. They were in the heart of the mountains now. Darek was keeping a sharp eye out for movement below. They were looking for the creatures that Darek had seen in Zantor's last mind message.

"There!" cried Rowena. She pointed to a clearing. Out of the corner of his eye, Darek saw a number of small shapes scurry into the scrub.

"Down!" he commanded.

The three dragons tipped their wings and circled down. Darek, Pola, and Rowena dismounted. The clearing was empty, but there were little sharp-toed footprints everywhere.

"Hello!" Darek cried. "Don't be afraid. We come in peace."

Pola gave a hollow-sounding laugh. "If they're watching," he said, "they're bound to be frightened. These masks would scare anyone."

"You're right," said Darek. "I'll take mine off, just for a minute." He pulled his mask off and pushed back his hair. To his amazement he heard murmurs of surprise and delight all around him.

"It be him!" the creatures were calling to one another. "Dragon Boy be back!" A number of small, gray-scaled creatures emerged from the underbrush. One of them came forward. "Welcome, me friend!" he said with a wide, yellow-toothed grin.

"Who are you?" asked Darek. Then he looked around at the other creatures and added, "*What* are you?"

"Me, Zooba," said the one who had stepped forward. "Me be Dragon Boy's friend. Ye fix me leg. Me fix ye leg." Zooba pointed to a dark scar on his thigh. Then he swept his hand toward his friends. "We be Zynots. Remember ye now?"

"My name is not Dragon Boy. It's Darek," Darek told the little creature. "And these are my friends, Pola and Rowena. I'm afraid we don't remember much about our last visit."

"Ahhh." Zooba made a high, twittering sound

that Darek guessed to be laughter. "That be because of potion. Azzon took memories."

"Azzon?" said Darek. "Who's Azzon?"

"Azzon King of Krad," said Zooba. He put out a small, lizardlike hand. "Take you there."

"No, no!" said Darek quickly. "We don't want to go to Krad. Not yet anyway."

"Azzon not in Krad," said Zooba. "Azzon here."

"Here?" repeated Darek. This concerned him. He had thought they would be safe from the Kradens as long as they stayed in the mountains.

"Yes," said Zooba. "Come."

The clearing was full of Zynots now, all murmuring together and staring at the newcomers. Smaller ones, children probably, climbed all over Zantor and the other two dragons, petting them and chattering excitedly.

Darek looked up into Zantor's eyes. "You all right?" he asked as a little Zynot crawled out on the dragon's nose.

"*Thrummm,*" sang Zantor. Apparently he was fond of these creatures.

"Come," Zooba insisted, grabbing Darek's hand and tugging.

Darek gave a cough and replaced his mask. "No," he said again. "You don't understand. Kradens are our enemies. They'll hurt us."

"Azzon no hurt," said Zooba. "Azzon help."

7

Zooba led them deep under the mountains, through a steep, winding tunnel. Zantor, Drizba, and Typra and a gaggle of giggling zynots followed.

At last Zooba stopped. "Don't need masks now," he said. "Safe for ye here."

It was true. The dragonsbreath didn't seem to reach this far underground. Darek, Pola, and Rowena removed their masks and put them in their saddlebags. Zooba gave a small cough. "Go ye alone, now," he said. "Follow tunnel."

Darek stroked Zantor's neck. "The tunnel is getting narrow," he said. "You dragons stay here and play with your new little friends. We won't be long."

"*Rrronk,*" cried Zantor softly.

Darek smiled. "Don't worry," he said. "We'll be okay."

Darek, Pola, and Rowena went on alone. At last the tunnel widened into a cavern and they came to a great door.

"Guess this is it," whispered Darek.

"Guess so," said Pola.

Rowena nodded.

"Guess we should knock," said Darek.

"Guess so," said Pola.

Rowena nodded.

Darek stood staring at the great knocker.

"Well?" said Pola.

"Well what?" whispered Darek.

"Well, are you going to knock?"

Darek frowned. "Why do I have to do everything? Why don't you knock?"

"Me?" Pola protested. "What are you talking about? I do as much as you . . ."

"Oh, for pity's sake," snapped Rowena. Before either boy could say another word she grabbed the great knocker and slammed it down.

"KABOOM . . . BOOM . . . BOOM . . . BOOM!" The sound bounced around the cavern and echoed far back into the tunnel.

Instantly the door flew open and a fierce, hairy face stared down at them. For a moment, the tall, graying man seemed taken aback. Then his brows crashed into a deep V.

"You!" he bellowed. "I thought I had seen the last of you!"

Darek, Pola, and Rowena huddled together.

"You . . . you know us?" Darek stammered.

"Know you? Who do you think nursed you back to health and took you home?"

"You?" Darek's eyes widened in surprise. "But . . . the Zynots said you were the King of Krad."

"The *exiled* King of Krad," Azzon boomed. "Remember?"

Darek swallowed hard. "We remember very little," he said.

This seemed to calm Azzon. He stared at them, pulling thoughtfully at his beard. "So, the potion *did* work," he said after a time. "But, then, how came you back again?"

Darek swallowed hard. He didn't know if he

should trust this man. But the Zynots said he would help, and it seemed he had helped before . . .

"*How?*" Azzon bellowed. "Tell me before I feed you to the Red Fangs!"

Darek jumped. "The dragon showed us," he said.

"Dragon?" Azzon's eyes narrowed. "What dragon?"

Suddenly there was a heavy rumble of footsteps. Then a commotion of huffing and puffing, scratching and scraping, shrieking and giggling. And then into the cavern thundered Zantor, a dozen little Zynots still clinging to his back.

A smile tugged at Darek's lips. Zantor must have heard the *boom* of the knocker and gotten worried. "*That* dragon," he said.

Zantor had a wild look in his eyes, but when he saw Darek he grew calm. He loped over, then *thwippp!* Out flicked his tongue, planting a kiss on Darek's cheek.

Azzon stared openmouthed at the gentle blue

giant. Then he shook his head, and his anger seemed to melt away. "Now I've seen everything," he said.

The Zynot children twittered merrily.

"All right," said Azzon in a kindly voice. "Home with you now before you take ill." He plucked the Zynots off Zantor one by one. Giggling and tumbling over each other, they scurried back up the tunnel.

Now it was Darek, Pola, and Rowena who stared in wonder. Could this kindly old man truly be the King of Krad? Kradens were supposed to be fierce and cruel.

Azzon looked after the Zynots wistfully. "Would that they *could* stay and play," he said softly, almost to himself.

"Why can't they?" asked Darek.

"Their bodies have adapted to the dragonsbreath," said Azzon. "It's all they can breathe now."

"What did they breathe before?" Pola asked.

"The same thing you breathe," said Azzon. "In the Long Ago they were Zorians, like you."

Darek, Pola and Rowena gaped at Azzon.

"We're related to *them?*" asked Rowena.

"Yes," said Azzon, "but enough about Zynots. Why are you here?"

"Our fathers are somewhere in Krad," said Darek. "And my brother, too. We've come to rescue them."

"Ahhh." Humor glittered in Azzon's eyes. "And how do you propose to do that?"

"We're not sure," said Darek. "We thought you might help us."

"I?" Azzon chuckled. "Why would I turn against my own sons and help you?"

"Your sons?" Rowena repeated.

"Yes." Azzon sighed. "My sons rule Krad now, Zahr here in the north, and Rebbe in the south. But I've told you all this before. Come. For all the good the memory potion has done, I might as well give you the antidote. But first you must give me your word that you will never do anything to bring harm to my sons."

Darek, Pola, and Rowena glanced at one another in surprise. How could *they* possibly harm Azzon's sons?

"Agreed?" Azzon asked.

Darek shrugged. "Of course. You have my word."

"Mine too. And mine," added Pola and Rowena. Then the three followed Azzon into a large, torchlit cave. Zantor squeezed through the door right behind them.

"Aack, aack," came a small cough.

Darek looked up to see a small Zynot still perched, like a crown, on the top of Zantor's head.

"Mizzle!" cried Azzon. "Down from there this minute!"

Mizzle slid down Zantor's back and off his tail, twittering wildly.

"Out of here. Now!" shouted Azzon. He swatted playfully at the child's rear as it scurried out the door.

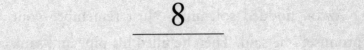

8

Azzon's antidote worked like magic. For the first time in months, Darek felt himself again. There were no empty gaps anymore. No more questions unanswered. He remembered all about Azzon now. How his two sons had turned against each other, and then against him. How Azzon had nearly died, fleeing into the Black Mountains. How the Zynots had rescued him and brought him to this cave, deep underground.

"This is wonderful!" cried Rowena. "I remember everything!"

"I, too," Pola agreed.

"Thank you, Azzon," said Darek. "We are grateful."

Azzon nodded solemnly. "Just remember your promise," he said. Then he filled his pipe and sank into a chair. He motioned to Darek, Pola, and Rowena to be seated as well. Then he lit his pipe and puffed quietly.

Zantor was snuffling around the room, exploring. Darek looked around, too. It was a great, dark cave, lit by torches. But it was quite richly furnished. How did Azzon come by such things here, underground? he wondered. Azzon caught his eye and seemed to read his mind.

"You like my decor?" he asked with a smile.

"Yes," said Darek, "it's . . ."

"Surprising," Rowena put in.

Azzon chuckled. "The Zynots are not so dull-witted as one might think," he said. "Every year, about this time, when the days grow warm and the ground is still cold, the dragonsbreath settles low into the valley at night, like fog. The Kradens and their Zorian slaves must stay inside with doors and shutters sealed tight. But the Zynots are free, as long as there is no wind or rain, to come down from their mountains. They scamper about, shrieking and moaning. They pummel the doors and rattle the shutters. It's really quite convincing."

"You mean . . . the Kradens think they are spirits?" said Pola.

"Yes." Azzon laughed. "I was humiliated when I found out the truth. All those years hiding in fear of a bunch of masquerading Zynots!"

"But . . . what has all that to do with your furnishings?" asked Rowena.

"Gifts," said Azzon. "The Kradens leave gifts of all sorts on their doorsteps. They try to outdo one another, hoping the spirits will be pleased and do them no harm."

"Ahhh!" Darek, Pola, and Rowena laughed.

"You seem fond of the Zynots," said Pola.

Azzon nodded. Then his face grew grave. "We Kradens have been merciless to the Zynots," he

said. "We've killed and maimed them, just for sport, whenever we've caught them down in the foothills.

"They had every right to kill me when they found me. Instead, they brought me to this cave and risked their own lives to care for me. I was so touched by their kindness, I became a changed man."

Darek, Pola, and Rowena had been listening quietly. Now Darek spoke up. "But . . . if you are changed, why won't you help us?" he asked. "Why are you still loyal to your sons?"

Azzon's eyes filled with pain. "I was a cruel father," he said. "I made my sons what they are, and I deserve what has befallen me. I do not blame them. I love them . . . more than ever."

Darek sat thinking, remembering all the problems he had caused *his* father, all the times he had disobeyed. And yet his father had risked everything to follow him into Krad. It was a powerful force—a father's love.

"The love you feel for your sons," Darek said

quietly, "is like the love our fathers feel for us. That's why they followed us here. That's why they are in trouble. Surely you can understand."

Azzon did not answer for a long time. Then he nodded slowly. "I *can* understand," he said. "But that doesn't mean I can help. And even if I could help you rescue them, I couldn't take you back to Zoriac again. I've filled in the tunnel I took you through last time."

"We'll go back the way we came," said Darek.

Azzon shook his head. "You can't," he said. "The dragonsbreath will addle your minds."

"No, it won't," said Darek. He walked over to Zantor and pulled a mask from the saddlebag. "We have these."

Azzon took the mask from Darek's hand. "What is it?" he asked.

"It's a mask that filters out dragonsbreath," Darek told him. "Our ancestors invented them, when they used to fight the Red Fangs."

Azzon stared at the mask in wonderment. "What is it made of?" he asked.

Darek shook his head. "We don't know," he said.

"But I'll bet my father does," Rowena put in. "He's the Chief Elder."

Azzon's brows arched up in surprise. "The Chief Elder of Zoriac is here? In Krad?"

"Yes." Rowena nodded. "He left his throne to come after me. I never dreamed he loved me that much."

The sadness came into Azzon's eyes again. "You are fortunate to have such fathers," he said. "Would that I had been such a father to my sons."

"Perhaps you still can be," said Darek. "It's never too late."

Azzon shook his head. "You don't know my sons," he said. "They were raised on the battle-field. Their lullabies were the screams of dragons in the gaming pits. They would as soon kill me as look at me."

Darek, Pola, and Rowena exchanged sorrow-ful glances.

"Do not pity me!" Azzon snapped. "I have

made my destiny. I am content to pay the price. My only concern now is, what am I to do with you?"

Zantor was still shuffling around the room, poking his head into this and that, snuffling and sniffling. Now there came a sudden crash and they all jumped.

"*Zatz!*" shouted Azzon. "Look what your beast has done!"

Zantor had upset a shelf high up on the wall. Bottles, jugs, and beakers tumbled to the floor.

"Sorry!" cried Darek. "He didn't mean anything. He was probably just looking for something to eat."

"Dratted dragon!" Azzon shouted. "Those are my potions!" He strode across the room and knelt beside Zantor, trying to salvage what he could. Darek ran over to try and help. Then suddenly he stopped in his tracks. Zantor was shrinking!

"Zantor!" he cried. "What's happening?"

Azzon looked at the dragon. "Oh, he'll be all right," he said shortly. "He must have sampled

the youth potion. It will just make him younger for a while."

"Younger?" cried Darek. "For how long?"

Azzon shrugged. "A day. Maybe two. Depends how much he drank. Unless he gets upset or angry. That could get his blood racing and snap him out of it."

Darek looked at Zantor, who had shrunken down to the size of a newborn. He was sitting quite happily amidst the mess, looking anything but upset. In fact, he had his snout in another beaker!

"Oh no!" cried Darek. "Now what's he got?"

Azzon reached out and snatched the beaker away. He held it up to the light. Then he chuckled. "This one won't hurt him," he said. "But he's going to stink for a while."

9

Darek couldn't sleep. Zantor had insisted on crawling into bed with him, and the smell, like rotten eggs, was making him ill. Not only that. Each time Darek tried to move, little Zantor only snuggled closer. He *was* awfully cute, Darek had to admit, if not for the smell. But Darek hoped Zantor wouldn't stay small for long. They would need him for the rescue, whenever or however *that* happened. One thing was certain. Azzon was not going to help.

Darek felt a tug on his arm.

"Go to back to sleep, Zantor," he mumbled. "I'm here."

There was a little twitter near his ear. "Not Zantor," someone whispered. "Mizzle!"

Darek's eyes flew wide open. "Mizzle!" he whispered. "What are you doing here? You'll get sick."

"Know where fathers are," the small creature whispered.

"What?" Darek sat up.

"Sssss!" said Mizzle, pressing a skinny little finger to his lips. "Need be quiet."

"Why would you help us?" asked Darek. "I thought you were Azzon's friend."

"Mizzle be Azzon's friend," the little creature replied. "But Zooba be Mizzle's father. Ye helped me father. Me help ye father."

Darek smiled and nodded. Zantor poked his head out from under the blankets.

Mizzle looked startled. "Ye dragon?" he questioned.

"Yeah," Darek whispered. "He got into some

of Azzon's potions. Azzon said it will wear off in a day or two."

Mizzle pinched his nose. "Gleep," he said.

Darek nodded. "Yeah. Tell me about it!"

Mizzle giggled again. "Hurry," he said. "Follow."

"Go get Pola and Rowena," Darek told Zantor. "And be quiet about it." Zantor scurried away and Darek pulled his breeches on.

Pola and Rowena came in rubbing their eyes. "What's going on?" they asked.

"Mizzle knows where our fathers are," said Darek. "Grab the masks and let's go."

It was dark and damp and hard to see. The mists swirled as thickly in the valley this night as in the mountains. Mizzle led them carefully past the great cage where the Kradens' fierce Red Fanged dragons slept. Darek shivered, looking at the giant beasts so close on the other side of the fence. One rolled over and belched a stream of fire into the

night and Darek and the others nearly fell over
each other in their haste to get away.

As they drew closer to the village they heard
a fierce din of shrieking and moaning. Darek's
skin prickled. Suddenly a dark shape flew out of
the night, almost bowling them over. It made a

hideous face and waved long, sharp claws. It danced around them for a moment, howling and flailing its claws, then ran off toward the village, cackling wildly.

"What was *that?*" cried Darek.

"Night Spirit," said Mizzle with a giggle.

"Lord," whispered Rowena. "No wonder the Kradens bar their doors."

Up ahead the dark battlements of Castle Krad loomed. Darek's heart beat faster. Night Spirits or no, he didn't like passing so close to that wicked place. Inside its walls lived the evil Zahr. A shift in the wind or a sudden shower and Zahr's men would be free to patrol the streets again.

"I don't like this," Pola whispered.

Darek and Rowena nodded their agreement.

Zantor seemed unconcerned. He frolicked up ahead with Mizzle, while Drizba and Typra brought up the rear.

When they reached Castle Krad, Mizzle suddenly dashed up to the great doors and pounded on them. He lifted his head and gave an ear-splitting shriek. Darek's heart raced. Was Mizzle betraying them?

"Mizzle!" he cried. "What are you doing? Do you want to get us all killed?"

Mizzle rushed back to them, twittering wildly. "Mizzle scare Zahr!" he cried, clapping his little hands. "Mizzle funny."

"Mizzle not funny!" said Darek. "Mizzle foolish!"

Mizzle hung his head. "Mizzle sorry. Mizzle love Spirit Night," he mumbled.

Darek couldn't help smiling. "Mizzle," he said gently. "Our fathers, remember?"

Mizzle looked up and grinned again. "Fathers, yes!" he cried, scampering off again.

They followed Mizzle toward a group of low hills in the distance. As they got closer, Darek could make out a dark opening in the hillside.

Mizzle pointed. "Mines," he said.

"Our fathers are in there?" asked Rowena.

"Men slaves work mines," said Mizzle. He stretched his hand up high. "Big boys too. Small boys work dragons."

"Yes." Darek nodded. He and the others remembered everything about their slave days now.

They were approaching the opening. A great door stood barred across it.

"Keep out Night Spirits," said Mizzle with a giggle.

"How will *we* get in?" Pola asked.

"Come," said Mizzle. "Be quick." He pointed to the sky. "Daylight come soon. Burn off mist." He scampered up the steep hillside with Zantor close on his heels. Darek followed. He found them at the crest, staring down at a small, square opening.

"What is it?" asked Pola and Rowena as they came up behind.

"Looks like an old air shaft," said Darek. "But it's sealed and there are bars across it."

"I'll get Drizba's tether," Rowena offered. "We can tie one end to the grate and let her pull it free."

"Great idea," said Darek.

Mizzle howled his loudest to cover the noise, and in no time at all the grate was out. The group pried off the lid and knelt around the opening. They could see a light flickering below and hear the murmur of voices.

"Guards," said Mizzle.

"We've got to distract them," said Pola.

"Me get Zynots," said Mizzle. "Make much noise."

"That'll help," said Darek, "but we've got to get them out of that room down there somehow." He lifted his mask to scratch his nose and Zantor's stench nearly made him gag.

"Zatz, Zantor, you stink!" he whispered.

"That's it!" cried Pola.

"What's it?" asked Darek.

"You'll see," said Pola. "Rowena, get Drizba's tether again."

10

Zantor dangled from the end of the tether, inside the shaft, just above the guard's room. He stared up at Darek, Pola, and Rowena with mournful eyes.

"Shush," Darek begged him, pressing a finger to his lips. "Don't make a sound, okay?"

Rrronk, came a loud and clear mind message.

Darek smiled. "It shouldn't be much longer," he whispered.

Sure enough, a moment later he heard one of the guards say, "Phew! What *is* that smell?"

"I don't know," another one replied. "Zatz! It smells like something died!"

"Aargh! I can't take it," a third put in. "I've got to get out of here."

There was a murmur of agreement, a scraping of chairs, and then silence. Darek grinned down at Zantor. "Good job!" he whispered.

Thrummm, came the soft reply.

"EEEyiiiooowwll!! Arrooogh!! Grraahrr!!" Mizzle was back with his friends and they were setting up a mighty din.

"Let's go," whispered Darek.

Slowly they lowered Zantor to the floor of the room, then one by one they slid down the rope to join him. Darek untied Zantor, who greedily attacked a bowl of fruit on the guard's table.

"Little guy's hungry," whispered Pola. "Come to think of it, so am I."

"Forget it, Pola," said Darek. "We've got more to worry about than our stomachs." He pushed his mask back and looked around. One tunnel led upward away from the room, and another down.

"Which way?" he whispered.

"My guess would be down," said Rowena.

Pola nodded. "Mine too."

"All right," said Darek. "Let's go." He grabbed a torch from the wall and led the way into the tunnel.

"Hey," cried Rowena. "Look what *I* found." She reached up high on the wall and took down a heavy ring of keys.

Darek and Pola grinned. "This is almost too easy," said Pola.

"Don't count your zoks before they hatch," Darek warned.

The tunnel was narrow and dank. Water oozed out of the walls and the floor was slimy with mold. The deeper they went, the colder it became.

Darek shivered. "I hate to think of our fathers living down here," he said.

"Or the other Zorian slaves," said Rowena quietly.

Darek swallowed. That *was* hard to think about. Just as it was difficult to think about Arnod and the other slave friends they had left behind on their last visit to Krad. They had promised to return and help those friends one day.

"Someday, somehow, we'll help them all," he whispered. "But right now we've only got enough masks to get our fathers and Clep back through the mountains."

Pola and Rowena nodded in sad agreement.

"Listen!" Pola suddenly whispered.

They froze. Heavy footsteps were coming up the tunnel toward them. Darek looked around wildly, then remembered a small niche in the wall a short way back.

"Hurry!" he cried, dousing his torch.

The three ran back and crowded into the niche. Then they pulled Zantor in behind them, pinching their noses at his stench. Their hearts pounded as the steps came closer. Torchlight flickered farther down in the tunnel and then two guards came into view. Darek held his breath and tried to shrink further into the shadows as they clomped

by. Just then, Zantor let out a small belch. Darek's heart lurched.

"What was that?" one of the guards asked.

"What?" asked the other. "I didn't hear anything."

"Ugh! What's that smell?" the first guard cried. Then, "Zatz, man! Is that you! What in Krad did you eat for dinner?!"

"It's not me," the second man cried. "It must be *you*, you sloth!"

Darek, Pola, and Rowena clapped their hands over their mouths to keep from laughing. They could still hear the two men arguing as their footsteps faded away.

"Phew," whispered Rowena, "that was close."

"Yeah." Pola nodded. "And now we've lost our light."

"Oh, no we haven't," said Darek. "You forget the many talents of our smelly little friend here." He lifted the torch. "Zantor," he said, "light, please."

11

Darek lifted his torch high and peered in through the small barred window of the cell door. Then he shook his head. "Not them," he whispered. He and the others were growing discouraged. They'd peeked into dozens of cells but had yet to find Clep or any of their fathers among the sleeping slaves.

"It'll be dawn soon," said Rowena. "We're running out of time."

"We'd better get back," said Pola. "It won't help anything if we're captured."

Pola was right, Darek realized, but . . . they

were so close! "Just a few more cells," he said. "Then we'll go." He crept up to the next door and peered in, then the next, then his mouth dropped open. "It's them!" he cried.

Pola and Rowena scrambled to get a peek.

"Praise Lord Eternal," Rowena whispered, tears filling her eyes.

"Try the keys," cried Darek. "Hurry!"

Rowena took out her keys and fumbled with the lock. Several didn't work, and then one turned and the door swung open.

"Thrummm," sang Zantor. He flew by and leapt joyfully on Darek's sleeping brother.

"What the—"

"Shush!" cried Darek. He crouched at his brother's side. "Quiet, Clep. We've come to rescue you."

Clep's eyes grew wide. "Darek!" They grabbed each other in a rough hug. "Lord Eternal! I thought I'd never see you again!"

The fathers were carefully wakened as well, and after a quick round of hugs and tears, Darek pressed them to get going.

"Who's the little dragon?" his father asked. "And why does he smell so bad?"

"It's Zantor," said Darek with a soft laugh. "I'll explain later. If we don't get out of here before the sun comes up, the Kradens will be able to follow us. Hurry!"

"What of the other slaves?" asked the Chief Elder.

"We have no way of getting them through the mountains," said Darek. "If we free them now, they'll only perish."

The Chief Elder hesitated. "But they are Zorians, like us," he said. "They are our friends."

"Yes." Rowena took her father's hand. "And that is why we must escape while we can. So that one day we can return and help them."

The Chief Elder nodded. "Onward then," he said.

Darek led the way back, but as they approached the guards' room once again they heard a din of excited voices. Someone was shouting orders to search the tunnels! They had been discovered.

"This way," said Darek's father, hurrying to the front of the group. "We'll have to make a run for the main entrance." He led the way down another passage and Darek followed willingly. It felt good, for the moment, to be a kid again, to let his father take control.

The passage twisted this way and that. Soon they heard shouts and pounding footsteps behind them.

"Run faster!" came Clep's voice from behind.

Darek's breath was already coming in ragged puffs, but he pushed himself even harder. Pola and Rowena were close on his heels, and Zantor fluttered overhead. Clep and the other fathers brought up the rear. At last the tunnel began to widen. Darek could hear the howling of Mizzle and his Night Spirits in the distance.

"We must be near the entrance," Darek cried over his shoulder.

Sure enough, they rounded a bend and there stood the huge wooden doors. The way to freedom!

Then Darek's father stepped aside and Darek saw that between them and the doors stood a dozen armed guards.

12

Darek tried to turn back, but it was too late. More guards were already herding Pola, Rowena, and the others into the center of the room. They all huddled together, downcast, and breathing heavily. Zantor seemed to sense Darek's despair.

"*Rrronk,*" he cried softly.

"Well, well," said one of the guards. "What have we here? A family reunion? How cozy."

Outside, Darek could hear Mizzle and the others still howling and shrieking. He swallowed hard and looked down. They had come so close to freedom. *So close!* Tears stung his eyes.

One of the guards stepped forward. "I know these three," he said. "These are the three whelps that escaped from the dragon nurseries a while back."

Darek looked up—into the eyes of Daxon, Master of the stockyards. Daxon's eyes narrowed.

"That's right, boy," Daxon said. "It's me. Your old Master. Thanks to you I've been demoted to mine guard." He laughed wickedly. "Now I'll have a chance to redeem myself."

Daxon stepped forward and grabbed Darek by the shoulders and started to shake him. Out of the corner of his eye, Darek saw his father rush forward. But another guard shoved him aside.

"Rrronk, rrronk!" cried Zantor. He flew up and clawed at Daxon, but Daxon brushed him off like a flea. "Kill that dragonling!" he bellowed to the other guards.

"Rrronk, rrronk!" Darek heard Zantor cry as several guards grabbed for him.

"No!" Darek shouted. "Please!" But then a

powerful blow stung him across the cheek. He tasted blood in his mouth.

"Rrronk, rrrOWK, GRRAWWWK!" Darek heard. Then suddenly there came a great thrashing and crashing. Guards went flying and a burst of flame flashed above Darek's head, scorching Daxon's beard.

"Aagh!" Daxon cried. He let go of Darek and began to beat at the flames.

Darek turned. Zantor was full size again, and angrier than Darek had ever seen him! Guards flew left and right. Weapons clattered to the floor. Bursts of flame flashed around the room like lightning. With cries of terror the guards gathered up their fallen comrades and ran for the tunnel.

"Zantor!" Darek cried. "The doors! Hurry!"

With a scream of fury, Zantor turned and hurled himself at the heavy doors. They splintered like tinder, spilling him out into the night.

"C'mon!" Darek motioned to the others. "Follow me!"

Out they rushed, one and all, into the waiting arms of the Night Spirits.

13

Darek, Pola, and Rowena stood beside their dragons. Their fathers were at their shoulders, and Clep at Darek's side. Darek couldn't see the others' faces behind their battle masks, but their eyes danced with joy. Even the Black Mountains seemed cheerful today.

"Well," said Darek's father proudly. "It seems that you've proven yourself a hero once again, my son."

Darek blushed and glanced at the throng of Zynots who had come to say good-bye. "I'm not the hero, Father," he said. He stroked Zantor's neck and looked up at Mizzle, who sat perched on the dragon's head. "These two are the heroes."

Zantor *thumm*ed softly, and Mizzle twittered.

Zooba grinned. "Come ye down here, son," he called.

Mizzle slid down Zantor's back into his father's arms. Darek removed his mask for a moment and reached a hand out to the little Zynot. "How can I ever thank you, my friend?" he asked.

Mizzle grinned. "No need thank Mizzle," he said. "Mizzle be glad ye be with ye fathers. All be happy now, like Mizzle and Zooba." He smiled up into his own father's eyes.

"Yes." Darek glanced at Clep and his father. They *would* be happy now. They were on their way home. Home to Zoriac, the farm, and Mother. All would be happy. All except the slaves they were once again leaving behind. And Azzon. For a moment Darek's mood darkened. He silently renewed his vow to fulfill his promise to the slaves one day. That was all he could do just now. And as for Azzon . . . Suddenly Darek had a thought.

"Rowena," he cried. "Do we still have that spare mask?"

Rowena nodded. "Yes," she said. "It's in Drizba's saddle bag."

"Can you toss it to me?" asked Darek.

Rowena shrugged and pulled out the mask. She tossed it to Darek, who caught it and handed it to Mizzle.

"Azzon may not be able to be with his sons," Darek said. "But at least he can be with his friends. With this on he can spend as much time up here with you as he likes."

Mizzle took the mask, put it on, and started dancing around. "Azzon be glad," he cried. "Zynots be glad, too."

He looked so comical in the oversized mask that Darek and the others couldn't help laughing.

"Good-bye, little Night Spirit," said Darek with a wink.

"*Grraahrr!*" cried Mizzle, flailing his arms.

Then he took off the mask and raised his hand in farewell. " 'Bye, Dragon Boy. Come ye back some day!"

Darek nodded, then climbed into his saddle and helped his father and Clep up behind him.

"Home, Zantor," he said softly.

Thrummm, sang the dragon. *Thrummm, thrummm, thrummm.*

Prologue

When Darek decided to rescue a baby Blue dragon from certain death, he had no idea that he was about to change his world forever. Darek's friendship with Zantor the dragon has brought one problem after another—problems with family, problems with friends, problems with Darek's whole village. But now it has led to the biggest problem of all.

When Zantor and Darek's best friend, Pola, disappeared into the dreaded Black Mountains of Krad, Darek and his friend Rowena went after them. The fathers of the three children and Darek's brother, Clep, soon followed. For a time all were enslaved in Krad. But with the help of Zantor, they finally escaped, only to be arrested upon their return to Zoriac. It is against the law for Zorians to venture into the Black Mountains. The law was made to keep Zorians from danger, and to be sure they did not disturb the mythical Kradens whom some believed lived there.

Darek and the others have discovered that the cruel Kradens are indeed real and that they keep Zorians as slaves. Darek and the others hope to go back and rescue the slaves, but first they must stand trial.

Darek, Pola, and Rowena are soon pardoned. They are only ten, too young to be sentenced. But their fathers and Clep face imprisonment, or even death. Especially if Zarnak has his way. Zarnak has been acting as Chief Elder while Rowena's father, the true Chief, has been away. It is a job Zarnak would like to keep. Now the trials are under way and the whole village waits. How will the Elders decide?

1

Something bumped Darek's back and he shot up in bed, wide awake, heart pounding. A forked tongue flicked out and kissed him on the cheek. Darek smiled and gave a sigh of relief.

"Oh, it's you, Zantor," he said. "Sorry I'm so jumpy. I didn't sleep much last night, worrying about the trial."

"*Grrrawwk,*" said Zantor.

Darek rubbed the gentle dragon's nose. Zantor was fully grown now, too big to fit in the house anymore. Instead, he camped under Darek's win-

dow at night and awakened Darek each morning
by pushing his great head in through the window.
His voice had changed too. His baby distress cry
of "Rrrronk" had become a full-throated
"Grrrawwk," and his joyful *thrummm*s were so
loud now they shook the house.

Zantor nudged him again, as if to say, "Let's
go."

"I'm not in the mood for a ride this morning,

Zantor," Darek said quietly. "Today the verdicts will be announced."

"*Grrrawwk,*" said Zantor, hanging his head. He looked so sad that Darek relented.

"All right," he said. "Just a short one."

Zantor's eyes lit up. "*Thrummm,*" he sang.

"Shussh." Darek couldn't help giggling as his bed started to vibrate across the floor. "You'll bounce Mother right out of bed." He slipped into his breeches, then threw his arms around Zantor's neck.

"Let's go," he cried.

Zantor ducked out of the window, then unfurled his silver wings. With one spring of his great legs they were airborne. Up, up they rose, until Darek's house looked like a little toy. Zoriak's violet sun was warm on Darek's back. Clean, fresh air filled his lungs and whipped at his hair. It was so good to be home, free from the gray, smoky skies of Krad. They circled the barnyard and struck off across the valley. In the morning stillness of a pond below, Darek caught sight of

Zantor's reflection. He was magnificent! Darek couldn't help smiling as he recalled the day he had given the tiny, trembling dragonling his name. "I will give you a strong name," he remembered saying, "a powerful name. I will call you Zantor, King of the Dragons." It had seemed back then that the name would never fit. Now it fit perfectly. Zantor was everything a king should be. He was powerful and strong, but he was good, too. Not like Zarnak, who was trying to steal the throne from Rowena's father. Or Zahr, the terrible king of Krad.

Darek shivered, recalling his slave days in Krad. His heart grew heavy at the thought of the other slaves he had left behind. They still labored day and night for the cruel Zahr.

"If only Azzon were king again," Darek said half aloud. "Azzon would set them free." Azzon had once been king of all Krad. He had been cruel then, too—so cruel that he'd raised his sons Zahr and Rebbe like beasts. When they grew older they had turned on each other, then on him, and Azzon had fled into the Black Mountains. He would have died there in the poisonous mists, but the gentle Zynots who lived in the mountains had saved him. Their kindness had changed Azzon into a good and gentle man. Now Zahr ruled Krad in the north and Rebbe in the south, not knowing or caring that their father still lived in hiding beneath the Black Mountains.

Someday, Darek promised himself, he would go back and help his slave friends in Krad. But now he had more pressing worries. His father and brother were on trial, along with Pola's father and Rowena's. If found guilty they could be put to death, and the verdict would be decided this very day.

2

Darek felt very small seated at the great council table. Overhead the fierce faces of long-dead dragons glared at him. Their skins covered the walls. Their tails trailed across the ceiling. On either side of Darek sat Pola and Rowena, looking just as small and scared as he. Behind them, in a second row of chairs, sat their mothers.

"All rise," boomed a loud voice.

Darek jumped to his feet as Zarnak, the acting Chief Elder, strode into the room. Behind him came the Council of Elders. Last came Horek, the dep-

uty captain of the guards, leading Darek's father and brother, Pola's father, and Xylon, the Chief Elder.

Zarnak took his place upon the Dragon Throne while the Elders filed into the chairs on either side of the council table. Darek tried to read their stony faces. Yesterday, Zarnak had called for a guilty verdict. But which Elders supported Zarnak, and which Xylon? There was no way to know.

The prisoners were seated directly across the table from Darek, Pola, and Rowena. Then the Deputy Captain went and stood at attention beside the throne. Darek hated to see the man standing in his father's place. He glanced at Rowena and knew she was feeling the same way. She glared at Zarnak, who sat upon her father's throne.

"Please, Lord Eternal," Darek whispered to himself. "Let the verdict go in our favor."

Two heralds stepped through the great doors at the end of the room and lifted their horns.

"Ta-da-da-da-da-DA!" the horns sounded.

Then Zarnak stood and unfurled a scroll. Darek held his breath.

"The exalted Council of Elders," Zarnak droned, "has met and considered this case in accordance with the laws of Zoriac." An evil gleam came into his eyes, and Darek's heart sank. "A verdict has been returned," he went on. "Guilty as charged!"

Darek felt like a fist had slammed into his stomach. Behind him he heard a small cry escape his mother's lips. Rowena was less discreet.

"No!" she cried out, but a sharp look from her father silenced her.

None of the fathers flinched at the verdict, but Darek's brother, Clep, turned pale. It was a hard blow for a boy of thirteen. Darek saw tears in his brother's eyes. Tears started behind Darek's eyes, too, and he looked down so his father and Clep would not see.

"Furthermore and notwithstanding," Zarnak went on, "the Council has taken the following facts into account. Fact one: The first child, Pola, was carried into the Black Mountains by a runaway wagon against his will. Fact two: The second and third children, Darek and Rowena, entered the Black Mountains out of concern for the first child. Fact three: The four defendants entered the Black Mountains out of concern for all three children."

A sour look had settled over Zarnak's features, and Darek began to feel a glimmer of hope.

"In consideration of these facts," Zarnak announced, "the sentence is hereby reduced to imprisonment in the dungeons of Elder Hall for one anum."

Darek closed his eyes and sank back in his chair. A year in prison. It was still uncalled for, in his opinion, but it could have been so much worse. He felt his mother's hand on his shoulder and he reached up and squeezed it.

3

Zarnak announced the verdict in the village square that afternoon. Darek had hoped the villagers would protest the sentence, but they did not. He listened to the low buzz of conversation around him. It was a fair sentence, the people murmured. A law was a law, after all, and everyone, even a Chief Elder, had to pay some price for breaking one.

Darek sighed and turned to Pola and Rowena. "So what do we do now?" he asked.

"About what?" asked Pola.

"About Krad and the slaves," said Darek.

Pola and Rowena shook their heads. "We'll have to wait," said Rowena, "until our fathers are free again."

"Yes," Pola agreed. "It will probably take that long to plan a rescue anyway."

Darek nodded thoughtfully. "Come to think of it," he said, "that might work out perfectly. A year from now will be Spirit season again."

Rowena's and Pola's eyes brightened. Spirit season occurred each spring in Krad, when the weather grew warm and the ground was still cold. For a few nights the mountain mists settled low in the valleys. The Kradens were forced to stay indoors, but the Zynots, who breathed the mist, were free to come down out of the mountains. They ran through the dark streets shrieking and howling, terrifying the Kradens, who believed they were evil spirits.

"Yes!" Rowena cried. "That would be the perfect time! The Zynots could help us rescue the slaves!"

"We might just be able to pull the whole thing off without bloodshed," said Pola.

"THERE IS ANOTHER MATTER!" Zarnak suddenly boomed from the platform in the middle of the square. "ONE WHICH REQUIRES OUR IMMEDIATE ATTENTION."

The faces of the crowd turned upward again.

"As we now know," said Zarnak gravely, "the Kradens are real. They are not creatures of myth, but beings like us. They are large and dangerous, to be sure, but not invincible."

The crowd murmured and nodded.

"There is something more you must know," said Zarnak. "Something terrible." He paused, then went on in a loud, dramatic voice. "There are Zorians in Krad, Zorian slaves!"

A gasp went up from the crowd and voices began to buzz in astonishment.

Darek frowned. "Why is he telling them that now?" he whispered to Pola and Rowena. "Why get them all riled up while our fathers are in prison?"

"I don't know," Rowena returned worriedly, "but I'm getting a bad feeling."

"These people are our kin," Zarnak was shouting. "Blood of our blood, descended from common ancestors."

The buzzing of the crowd grew louder.

"They are being held in dire conditions," Zarnak went on. "They are whipped, beaten, made to labor day and night. Their children are torn from their arms and put to work as soon as they can walk!"

Fists began to be raised in the air.

"Free the Zorians!" one man shouted.

"Death to the Kradens!" another cried.

Rowena suddenly whirled. "Zatz," she said to Pola and Darek. "Don't you see what he's up to? *He* wants to rescue the Zorians. He wants to be a hero. . . ."

Pola and Darek stared at her, then nodded slowly. "So the people will make him Chief Elder," said Pola. "So he can gain the throne for himself before your father is free again!"

Zarnak went on shouting about the plight of the slaves. He was whipping the crowd into a frenzy.

"Wait!" Darek cried. "No! You can't do this!" But his voice was lost in the uproar. "Pola, Rowena," he cried. "Help me up onto the platform!"

Pola and Rowena linked hands and gave Darek a boost. He hoisted himself up onto the platform, then stood and waved his arms.

"Hear me!" he cried. "Please hear me!"

Zarnak cocked an eye in his direction. "Seize him!" he shouted to one of his guards.

"NO!" came a piercing cry from the crowd.

There was a sudden hush as Rowena's mother, the Grand Dame, strode forward. Behind her were Darek's mother and Pola's.

"What are you afraid of, Zarnak?" she asked, looking up. "Why won't you let the boy speak? He has been to Krad, after all. Have you?"

"She's right," someone shouted.

"Yes," cried another. "Hear the boy out!"

"As you wish, milady" said Zarnak through

clenched teeth. He tilted his head to the Grand Dame, then turned and glared at Darek. "Speak!"

Darek swallowed hard, then looked down at the crowd. "It's true that the slaves need help," he said. "But a rescue must be carefully planned. It will take time. . . ."

"How much time?" snarled Zarnak. "An anum perhaps?"

"Per-perhaps," said Darek.

"Nonsense!" Zarnak boomed. "The boy is speaking for his father, don't you see? And the Grand Dame for her husband. Of course Xylon and Yanek want us to wait. Of course *they* want to lead the rescue, to be the heroes! But what of the slaves who are dying even now? What of the Zorian children crying in Krad this very day? Can *they* wait? *Should* they wait while our would-be heroes serve their time in prison?"

The crowd heated up again. "No!" people shouted. "Free them now! Save the children! Death to the Kradens! Death to Zahr!"

"But you've never even been to Krad!" Darek

shouted to Zarnak. "You know nothing about it! How can you lead a rescue?"

Zarnak came over and put an arm around Darek's shoulders. He smiled down wickedly. "Very easily, my young friend," he said. "You and your dragon will guide me."

"I'll not guide you anywhere," Darek spat.

"Oh, I think you will." Zarnak lowered his lips until they were right next to Darek's ear. "You see, the Elders have decreed how much time your father and brother will spend in prison. But it's up to me *how* they spend it. And may I remind you, some of our prison cells are . . . shall we say . . . more *comfortable* than others?"

Darek's blood ran cold. He thought back to the day, not long ago, when he and Pola had sneaked into the dungeons of Elder Hall. He remembered all too clearly the dank, dark solitary confinement cells, barely big enough for a man to lie down in.

"You wouldn't," he said in a hoarse whisper.

Zarnak's mouth widened into an evil grin. "Oh, but I *would*," he said with a low, menacing laugh.

4

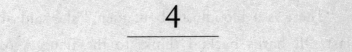

The village seemed flush with new life. Not since the days of the dragon quests had Darek seen so much activity. The women were busy making battle masks. The men were minting swords and stringing bows. The alehouses were full to bursting each night with men singing songs and telling tales of brave deeds of long ago.

"It's like they're happy," said Darek as he sat in the garden watching his mother stitch straps for the battle masks. "Don't they know how dangerous it's going to be? Don't they know they could be killed?"

Alayah sighed and dropped her hands in her lap. She looked into Darek's eyes and struggled to find the right words to say to him.

"There *is* a bloodlust about men," she said at last. "It harks back, I think, to the Long Ago, when men were little more than beasts and had to fight to live." She looked at a group of boys out in the lane, charging each other with wooden swords. "It sits in men's hearts like a smoldering ember," she went on, "ever waiting to be fanned into fury." Darek heard and knew the truth of his mother's words. He had felt that ember within his own young heart. Before Zantor came into his life, Darek had dreamed of joining a dragon quest. He had itched for the thrill of battle, longed to make the kill, and wear the prize, a dragon claw necklace, about his neck.

"*Grrrawwk,*" said Zantor softly. Darek put a hand on the dragon's head. They shared a special bond and often knew each other's thoughts.

"Don't worry, Zantor," he said. "Those days are behind me." He looked at his mother again.

"Men will die on both sides," he said quietly. "And there is no need. Only Zarnak's greed for power."

Alayah smiled sadly. "I fear, my son," she said softly, "that greed is at the root of most wars."

Darek stood up and paced the length of the garden. A guard, posted by Zarnak, watched his every move. Darek turned and paced back again.

"We've got to stop them," he said in a low voice. He quit pacing and turned to his mother. "Can't you do anything?" he asked. "You and the Grand Dame? Can't you talk to the other women?"

Alayah shook her head. "We're under guard, too, don't forget. Besides, the people believe Zarnak. They say we think only of your father and Clep. They say we must think of the slaves in Krad."

Darek bent and put his hands on the arms of his mother's chair. "I *am* thinking of the slaves," he said. "They'll die too. It's going to be a blood-bath. Don't you understand?"

Alayah's eyes filled with tears. "All too well," she said, looking away. "And you will be in the thick of it."

Darek bit his lip, angry with himself. His mother had enough on her mind. He hadn't meant to burden her further. He took her hands and squeezed them. "Don't you worry about Zantor and me," he said gently. "We know how to take care of ourselves." Then he looked over at the dragon and added, "Don't we, boy?"

"Thrummm," sang Zantor. He swung his great head over and licked the tears from Alayah's cheek.

There was a sudden clattering out on the street and another guard rode up. He dismounted and approached Darek.

"Your presence is required at Elder Hall," he said.

5

Pola and Rowena were already seated when Darek arrived. Zarnak was on the throne and Horek at his side.

"Ah, young Darek," said Zarnak in a falsely sweet voice. "We've been waiting for you. Do sit down."

Darek slid into a chair across from Rowena. *What is this all about?* he asked her with his eyes.

I have no idea, her eyes replied.

A glance from Pola told Darek he was equally puzzled.

"I suppose you're all wondering why you're here," said Zarnak.

Darek, Pola, and Rowena said nothing.

"Come, come now," said Zarnak. "This hostility will get us nowhere." He smiled wickedly. "Can't we all be friends?"

The three glared at him in silence.

"All right then," Zarnak snapped. "Have it your way. But you *will* cooperate, like it or not! We are going to Krad and you are coming with us. And we are *not* coming home without the slaves. So wipe those scowls off your faces and let's get down to business."

Darek, Pola, and Rowena glared on.

"Horek," boomed Zarnak. "The wretches need convincing. Get the prisoners—"

"No!" Darek leaned forward. "No," he said. "Leave the prisoners alone. We'll cooperate."

Zarnak arched a brow, then looked at Rowena and Pola. They both nodded.

"All right, then. Your fathers have told us much

about Krad. We need to know if they are speaking the truth."

Rowena frowned. "My father wouldn't lie," she snapped. "Do you think he would mislead his own people? Even to get back at you?"

"That remains to be seen," said Zarnak. "Now, tell me all you know of Krad."

Pola and Rowena turned to Darek. He took a deep breath and began. "Krad is a great basin," he said, "ringed on all sides by mountains. A thick mist of dragonsbreath clings to the mountains. This mist is deadly to Kradens and addles the minds of Zorians. Harmless little creatures called Zynots live in the mountains. They are descended from Zorians whose minds were addled long ago."

"Yes, yes," said Zarnak impatiently. "We know all that. The mist is of no concern as long as we wear our battle masks. I want to know about the Kraden forces. How strong are they?"

Darek and his friends exchanged glances.

"We have no idea how many men they have,"

he said. "Enough, to be sure. And we know nothing of the Southern Kingdom—the one Rebbe rules. There are slaves there, too. But we have only seen the Northern Kingdom—Zahr's."

"We will worry about the Northern Kingdom first," Zarnak said. "Once we have conquered Zahr we will turn our attention to Rebbe."

Darek's eyes widened. "Conquer?" he said. "You plan to *conquer* Zahr?"

"Of course," said Zarnak. "How else would we free the slaves?"

"There may be another way," Rowena put in.

Zarnak narrowed his eyes. "And what might that be?"

"If we could just wait for Spirit season . . ." she began.

"No waiting!" Zarnak boomed. "We leave as soon as possible." He turned back to Darek. "They say you're a natural-born leader," he said. "Tell me. How would *you* conquer Zahr?"

Darek shook his head. "I don't see any way," he said. "The Kradens are bigger and stronger than we are. And they have a powerful weapon—the Red Fanged dragons. We have but three fighting dragons in all Zoriac. Our Great Blues. One on one a Blue might be able to defeat a Red. But the Kradens have a herd of hundreds . . . . We don't stand a chance. Unless . . ."

Zarnak leaned forward eagerly. "Unless what?"

Darek sat back and chewed his lip thoughtfully. "Unless we capture the Red Fangs," he said.

Zarnak sat back, too. A slow smile curled his lips. "Horek," he said, "prepare our departure."

6

In two days' time all was in readiness. A battle force of over a thousand men was outfitted and eager to move out. The day of departure dawned bright and clear. Darek was to lead the way, on Zantor. Zarnak and Horek followed on Pola and Rowena's dragons, Drizba and Typra.

Pola, Rowena, and the rest of the men were to follow on yukes. Darek glanced at his two friends, beside their yukes, and saw the anger smoldering in their eyes. At least Darek was being allowed to ride Zantor. That was something to be grateful for.

"All mount!" came Horek's shouted command at last. Darek kissed his mother good-bye and she clung to him tightly for a moment. When she drew away, there were tears in her eyes.

"Stay well," she said softly.

"I will," Darek promised her. Then he grabbed the mounting rope that hung from Zantor's saddle and climbed up onto the dragon's back. He lowered his battle mask and patted Zantor's neck. "Well, old friend," he said, "as Pola always says, an adventure's an adventure, all the way to the end. Looks like we're on our way again."

The dragons flew slowly, keeping just ahead of the yukes. By late afternoon they had gained the mountain peak and begun their descent. "I'd suggest making camp here," Darek called out at dusk. "The lower we go, the thinner the mist. Soon the Kraden guards will be able to see us."

Zarnak nodded and gave the signal to land.

"Pass the word to your men," Darek told

Horek. "Tell them to take their masks off only long enough to eat. The mist sneaks up on you."

A guard brought Pola and Rowena forward.

"You'll camp with us," Zarnak told them. "I want the three of you where I can keep my eye on you."

Rowena snorted. "Aren't we lucky," she said. She yanked her arm out of the guard's grip and sat down on a log. "When do we eat?" she asked. "I'm starving."

Zarnak chuckled, then handed her a pot and a plucked zok. "Just as soon as you cook," he said. "I do so enjoy food prepared with a woman's touch."

"Really?" said Rowena. She flung the zok back in Zarnak's face. "There, I touched it. Enjoy!"

Zarnak lunged and grabbed her arm. "Look, you little wench," he said. "You may be used to getting your own way. But those days are over. *I'm* Chief Elder now."

"No, you're not," snapped Rowena. "Not as long as my father lives."

Zarnak chuckled. "You'd best behave," he said in a low voice. "Or that may not be very long." Then he jerked her to her feet and handed her the zok again. "Make a stew," he said. "And don't get any funny ideas. We'll all be eating out of the same pot."

Then he turned and pointed To Darek and Pola. "Make a campfire!" he bellowed.

Under the watchful eye of a guard, Darek and Pola set about gathering sticks. Then Darek called Zantor to breathe on the pile. Soon Rowena's stew was bubbling. She ladled it into bowls and passed it around and they all began to eat.

"What was that?" Zarnak suddenly asked.

"What?" asked Darek.

"I thought I heard something." Zarnak looked around warily. "I get the feeling something is watching us."

"Something is," said Darek. "Lots of some-things. The Zynots. They're wondering who you are and what you want."

"Why don't they show themselves?" asked Zarnak.

"They don't trust you," said Darek.

"They're good judges of character," Rowena added.

Pola and Darek smiled into their bowls.

Zarnak snorted and went back to his meal. "Well, if they know what's good for them, they'll stay out of my way," he said.

"They will," boomed a sudden loud voice. "But I won't!"

Zarnak dropped his plate and stared up at the huge masked figure that had just emerged from the mist.

7

_____

"Azzon!" cried Darek, Pola, and Rowena at once. They all jumped up.

Zarnak jumped up, too.

"You know this creature?" he demanded of Darek and his friends.

"Yes. He's the rightful King of Krad," said Darek.

Zarnak's eyes widened. "Take him prisoner!" he shouted to the guards. They closed in with spears raised. Suddenly out of the shadows leaped dozens of small, gray-scaled creatures. With loud

shrieks and howls they starting kicking the guards and throwing rocks at them. The guards began to thrust back at the creatures with their spears.

"STOP!" bellowed Azzon. He eyed the creatures angrily, but when he spoke there was a note of fondness in his voice. "Out of here, now!" he commanded, "before you get hurt."

Reluctantly, the creatures slipped back into the shadows. The guards closed in on Azzon again.

"No!" Rowena came forward and grabbed the nearest spear. "Azzon is a friend."

"*Was* a friend," said Azzon. He looked hard at Darek, Pola, and Rowena. Then he looked around him at the camp and the regiments that stretched back into the hills. "Friends don't break promises," he added quietly.

Darek's cheeks grew hot. Azzon had helped them many times. In return, they had promised never to bring harm to his sons.

"I'm sorry, Azzon," he said. "This is not our doing."

"Silence!" Zarnak interrupted. "What are you talking about? How do you know this Kraden?"

"If you'll allow Azzon to sit and eat with us," said Rowena, "I'll explain."

Zarnak pondered a moment, then nodded. The guards backed off enough for Azzon to sit down. Rowena then launched into the story of Azzon and his sons, and how Azzon came to be living beneath the mountain.

"Where did he get that battle mask?" Zarnak demanded.

"We gave it to him on our last trip," said Pola. "To thank him for his help. It allows him to spend time up here with the Zynots."

"That was foolish," said Zarnak. "What if he gave it to his sons? What if they—"

"As you have been told," Azzon interrupted, "I am estranged from my sons. They don't know I'm alive. If they did, they would kill me first chance they got."

Zarnak stared at Azzon and pulled at his chin thoughtfully. "In that case," he said, "perhaps you can be of use to us. You could help—"

"No," Azzon snapped. "I am to blame for what my sons are. I hold no anger toward them. I love them, and I will not be a party to your plans."

Zarnak frowned. "Chain him, then!" he shouted to the guards.

Darek, Pola, and Rowena watched helplessly as Azzon's hands and feet were locked into irons. Azzon would not even meet their eyes.

Scuffling and mumbling sounds were heard in the bushes.

Zarnak turned toward the sounds. "As for all of you!" he shouted.

"*Sire,*" said Darek loudly.

Zarnak whirled. "*What?*"

Darek walked over to Zarnak and spoke qui-

etly. "You'd be wise not to send the Zynots away," he said. "They know these hills better than anyone."

Zarnak stared at him thoughtfully. "Yes," he said. "You have a point." He turned toward the mist again. "Zynots!" he shouted. "If you don't wish to see your friend Azzon harmed, then I expect your full cooperation. Come forth now."

There was only silence. Zarnak pulled a dagger

from his belt and walked over to Azzon. He put it to the big man's throat.

"NOW!" he bellowed.

Slowly the Zynots began to emerge. A very small one sidled up to Darek and grabbed his hand. Darek looked down and smiled.

"Hello, Mizzle," he said.

8

Darek followed his old friend Mizzle down the dark mountainside. Zantor had been left behind, much to his dismay. His scent would have warned the Red Fangs of their approach. Following close behind Darek came Zarnak, Horek, and a couple dozen of their best warriors. Mizzle watched over his shoulder. Each time Zarnak dropped back out of earshot, he spoke.

"Mizzle no like Zarnak," he said quietly.

Darek smiled. "Me neither," he said. "But he's got all the power right now."

"What be power?" asked Mizzle.

"It's how people make others do things," said Darek.

"Power bad," said Mizzle.

"Not always," said Darek. "But it's bad if a cruel person has it."

"Like Zahr?" said Mizzle.

"Yes. Like Zahr, and Rebbe, and Zarnak. I'm beginning to think they're all cut from the same mold."

"But Zarnak not be Kraden," said Mizzle.

Darek nodded. "I know. But it seems that perhaps Kradens and Zorians aren't so . . ."

"So what?" asked Mizzle.

"So different," Darek added thoughtfully. "So different after all."

"How close are we?" came a loud whisper.

"Be close," Mizzle called to Zarnak. "Be very close."

They began to hear the rustlings of the sleeping dragons. An occasional belch of flame brightened the night. At last the great cage loomed before them. Darek's heart thumped. The Reds were beautiful, their scales glowing pure white in the moonlight. They looked peaceful in sleep. Only their bloodred fangs gave away their fierce nature.

Mizzle coughed. "Guards be there, there, and there." He pointed, then coughed again.

"Thanks, little friend," said Darek. "You'd better get back now. The mist isn't thick enough for you here."

"Good luck, Dragon Boy," said Mizzle. "Be ye careful."

"I will," said Darek. But inside he was frightened. He knew he'd be lucky to get through this night alive.

Mizzle scurried away into the darkness, just as Zarnak and Horek came up.

"Where are they?" Zarnak asked.

Darek pointed out the guard positions. Zarnak nodded, then sent Horek and the men forward. Zarnak and Darek watched as the men slipped through the shadows toward the unsuspecting guards.

"They'll never know what hit them," Zarnak said with a chuckle.

Darek swallowed hard. He should be glad. The Kradens had been cruel to him and to the other slaves. But his own words kept echoing in his ears. *Perhaps Kradens and Zorians aren't so different after all.* Maybe there were good Kradens and bad Kradens, just like there were good and bad Zorians. What if some of these men were the good ones? What if they were fathers, with children waiting at home? What if . . .

Darek heard a gasp and a strangled cry. Then another. One by one the dark shapes of the Kradens slumped to the ground. Darek swallowed again and looked away.

Horek scrambled back up the hill. "The guards are taken care of, sire," he said. "But we'd better move fast. No telling when the watch changes." Zarnak nodded. The plan was to get the dragons out of the cage and up into the mountains where the Kradens couldn't follow. Darek, who had a way with dragons, was to go in first and try to get a harness on the lead male. If he was successful, the other dragons would follow. If he failed . . . Darek sucked in a deep breath. No sense dwelling on what would happen if he failed.

"Ready, *Dragon Boy?*" Zarnak asked sarcastically.

Darek didn't smile. He followed Horek down the hill to the cage. The Reds were waking up, aroused by the scuffle with the guards, no doubt. They paced fretfully in their cage, sniffing the air, bellowing their anger at being disturbed. Soon their roars would be heard in town. Then Zahr's men would ride out to investigate. Time was growing short.

Horek handed Darek a harness. "When we pull the doors open," he said, "you go in. The lead male will be the first to approach."

Darek nodded, then slung the harness over his shoulder.

"Open the doors," he said.

9

Darek willed his heart to stop pounding. The dragons would sense his fear. He had to remain calm. The herd had backed off upon his entrance. They milled fretfully, tossing their heads, snorting an occasional blast of flame. Darek watched, trying to pick out the lead male, trying to be ready when the beast made its move. Just then one of the largest males locked eyes with him. Darek stared back, trying not to flinch. He attempted to send a mind message, the way he did with Zantor, a calm, soothing mind message.

The male moved toward him, slowly. *Easy,* Darek said with his mind. *Easy. I won't hurt you.* The beast came on, head down, eyes fixed on Darek's. Slowly Darek slid the harness off his shoulder and held it out.

"Easy," he said softly. "We're just going to take a little ride."

Then, without warning, the dragon reared! When it crashed down again, flames shot from its mouth. Its eyes blazed. Darek froze.

GRRAWWWK! screamed the beast. Then it charged!

It all happened so fast, Darek couldn't think. First the blast of flame. Then he was hurled into the air. His head hit the roof of the cage. But before he fell to the ground he was caught and whipped around once more. His neck snapped painfully. He saw claws slashing, fangs flashing. He flailed with his arms, kicked with his legs. But it was no use. His body was launched into the air again. This time he hit the side of the cage and crashed to the ground in a crumpled heap.

GRRAWWWK! Another earsplitting scream. Darek looked up but couldn't see. Blood ran in his eyes. With a trembling hand he wiped it away, waiting to see the Red bearing down again. Instead, he saw a blur of white and red . . . and blue!

"Zantor!" he cried.

If Zantor heard him, he gave no sign. He couldn't. He was locked in a battle for his life. Darek watched with pounding heart as the dragons reared and charged, then reared and charged again. The other dragons watched, too, in hushed silence. This was a duel of kings. Bursts of fire flashed in the night. Screams of fury echoed off the mountains. The two clashed again, and when they came apart, both were bloodied.

Darek winced. Strange and terrible thoughts raced through his mind. Zantor's thoughts. Thoughts he'd never known the gentle creature capable of. The battle raged on. Both beasts were wounded. Both were tiring. Darek closed his eyes and prayed, prayed for the life of his beloved

friend. At last there came a piteous scream and Darek bit his lip. Slowly, he opened his eyes.

There on the ground lay the Red. His neck was pinned to the earth by Zantor's great jaws. His body was slack, but his great sides still heaved.

Darek received a terrible mind message. *Kill,* it said clearly. *Kill!* Darek closed his eyes and sent a message back.

No, Zantor, he said. *Don't kill. You have won. He is beaten. There is no need to kill.*

Slowly Zantor released his death grip. The Red struggled to its feet and dragged itself away. The other dragons closed in around Zantor and began licking his wounds. Clearly they had accepted him as their new leader.

Darek limped out and threw his arms around Zantor's bowed neck. "You *are* King of the Dragons, Zantor," he whispered. "But to me you're even more. You're the best friend anyone could ever have."

"*Thrummm,*" sang Zantor wearily. "*Thrummm, thrummm, thrummm.*"

10

The Red Fangs had followed Zantor willingly into the mountains and Zarnak was well pleased. So pleased that Darek dared to approach him the next morning as he stood watching the training exercises.

"Sire?" said Darek.

Zarnak looked down.

"Ah, young Darek," he said with surprising warmth. "How are your bruises this morning?"

"Better, sire, thank you."

"And the dragon? How is he?"

"Well, sire. Those Reds must have powerful

medicine in their tongues. His wounds are nearly
healed."

"Good. Good. He's quite a beast."

"Yes, sire." Darek smiled, then he shook his

head in wonderment. "I still can't believe the Reds accepted him that way."

"Oh, that's not so strange," said Zarnak. "The two breeds are very close. They've even been known to interbreed. Haven't you ever heard of Purple Spiked dragons?"

"Yes," said Darek. "Grandfather used to speak of them. But I never knew they were of mixed blood."

"They are. Part Red, part Blue."

Darek pondered this a moment. "It makes sense," he said at last. "My grandfather said they were very rare and very fierce."

"Yes." Zarnak sighed heavily. "Very fierce. My father and grandfather were killed by one, just days before I was born. I never knew either of them."

"I'm sorry," said Darek.

Zarnak nodded. "So am I. My grandfather was Chief Elder at the time. That's when the throne passed out of our family."

"Is that why you're so bent on getting it back?" asked Darek.

Zarnak stared straight ahead. "Yes," he said. "It belongs to me."

"But," Darek began, "you weren't born—"

"Enough!" snapped Zarnak. "You're spoiling my good humor. The past is past. I like the present better." He rubbed his hands together. "I gather from the noise and activity down in Krad that Zahr has discovered his empty dragon cage."

"Yes, sire," said Darek. "That's what I came to talk about."

"Oh?" Zarnak looked down at him again.

"Yes, sire. I was thinking that, without dragons, Zahr is in a very bad position."

"Yes." Zarnak chuckled. "Very bad indeed."

"So bad," Darek went on, "that he might be willing to talk."

"Talk?" said Zarnak. "Why would we want to talk? We've got the upper hand."

"But there will be bloodshed," said Darek. "Zahr is weakened without his dragons, but he

238

won't go down without a fight. And he'll take all the Zorians he can with him."

Zarnak did not seem concerned. "War is war," he said with a flick of his hand. "Men die."

Darek felt anger stir within him. *But not you, Zarnak,* he thought bitterly. *You will sit safe on your mountaintop and send others to their deaths.* He bit his tongue and turned to watch the training exercises. He knew many of these men. They were good men. Some of them were little more than boys. Back home their wives and mothers waited, praying prayers and shedding tears. How could Zarnak not care? Had his own loss hardened his heart? Did he think it only fair for others to suffer as he and his mother had? There must be some way to get to him. If not through his heart . . . then perhaps through his greed.

"You're right, Zarnak," said Darek. "Men do die in wars. But think what a hero you would be if all of these men came home safely. Imagine if you, Zarnak, could rescue the slaves without spill-ing a drop of Zorian blood. They would restore you to the throne for certain. They'd build monuments to you. Balladeers would sing your name. Why, Zoriak might even be renamed Zarnak."

Zarnak was listening now. He cocked his head and gave Darek a searching look.

"What do you have in mind?" he asked.

"Let me take Zantor and fly to Zahr's castle. Let me bargain with him. If he releases the slaves, we leave in peace."

"And what if Zahr decides to pursue us?"

"He can't. He can't get through the mist."

"He can if he figures out how to make battle masks."

"That could take years," said Darek.

"Or months. Or weeks." Zarnak shook his head. "No," he said firmly. "It's too risky. If we don't finish him now, we'll be forever looking over our shoulders."

11

Darek sat on a log between Pola and Rowena. The campfire flickered on their faces. Mizzle sat in the dirt by their feet, playing with a small, round stone. Zarnak came back from meeting with some of his men. He was in a jovial mood.

"Break out a barrel of slog," he called to one of the guards. "We shall celebrate tonight, for tomorrow Krad will be ours."

Tomorrow. Darek sighed heavily. He had hoped for more time to work on Zarnak, to get him to reconsider.

Azzon sat nearby, chained to a large rock. At Zarnak's words he had looked up briefly, then returned to staring sadly into the fire. *Poor Azzon,* thought Darek. *Up here away from his cave and his potions . . .*

Suddenly Darek's heart beat faster. Azzon's potions! Why hadn't he thought of them?

"Mizzle," he whispered under his breath.

Mizzle looked up at him.

"Don't look at me," said Darek. "Just listen."

Mizzle went back to playing with his stone, but he cocked an ear in Darek's direction.

"Go to Azzon's cave," said Darek. "Get the memory potion. Bring it back here. When no one is looking, dump it in the barrel of slog."

Mizzle sat quietly rolling his rock back and forth for another moment. Then he gave it an extra push and it started to roll down the mountainside. He scampered after it. Darek glanced at Pola and Rowena and smiled.

"What are you up to?" whispered Rowena.

"You'll see," said Darek.

Before long, Mizzle was back with the vial hidden under his arm. Dear Mizzle. He must have run like the wind. The barrel of slog had just been rolled up. Mizzle hopped around it, curiously. As soon as the lid was pried off, he jumped to the rim.

"Me try," he said, leaning over the foaming brew and pretending to drink.

"Zatz!" shouted Zarnak. "Get out of there!" Mizzle jumped down and scampered away, twittering merrily. "Glog good!" he cried. "Glog good." As he scampered past Darek, he winked one of his great, yellow-green eyes.

Zarnak called the guards up to dip their mugs. Then Zarnak dipped a mug for himself and sat down. Horek did the same. Zarnak lifted his mug to Horek's.

"To victory!" he said.

"To victory!" Horek returned. They clinked mugs and downed the glog.

"Ah," said Zarnak, wiping the foam from his mouth. "An excellent batch."

"Mmmm," Horek agreed, smacking his lips.

Darek watched closely. Before long Zarnak and Horek began to shrink! Their faces were growing younger and younger. Next moment Horek grabbed the crown off Zarnak's head.

"You always get to be Chief Elder," he cried in a whiny voice. "It's my turn now!"

"*No!*" Zarnak grabbed the crown back and they both started tugging.

Horek kicked dirt at Zarnak.

"Quit it, you meanie!" cried Zarnak. He pulled the crown free and whacked Horek over the head with it. All the while they were continuing to shrink. Soon two wailing toddlers sat tugging at their battle masks and struggling under a pile of oversized clothes.

Darek stared openmouthed. Azzon threw his head back and laughed.

"What the . . . ?" said Pola.

"How did you do that?" Rowena asked Darek.

Darek looked around at the guards, who had turned into toddlers, too. Then he started to laugh.

"I sent Mizzle for Azzon's memory potion," he said. "I told him to dump it in the slog. Looks like he brought the youth potion instead."

"Oop!" said Mizzle.

"No matter," said Darek. "This'll do the job. They won't be back to their normal selves for a couple of days."

"Probably even longer," said Azzon. "The alcohol in the slog will strengthen the potion."

"All the better," said Darek. "That'll give me plenty of time."

"To do what?" asked Rowena.

"To go see Zahr," said Darek. "To see if I can get him to surrender the slaves without bloodshed."

Azzon shook his head. "You're wasting your time," he said. "My son would rather die than surrender."

"Well, I've got to try," said Darek. "What is there to lose?"

"Your life," said Azzon. "Don't be a fool."

"A lot more lives will be lost if I don't try," said Darek. "Now, I've got to go. With the racket these babies are making, the other men will soon be up to investigate." He took a key from Zarnak's ring and unlocked Azzon's chains. Azzon pulled a ring from his finger and held it out to Darek. "Take this," he said. "Give it to Zahr. Tell him . . . tell him that I love him, and Rebbe, too. Tell him I'd like another chance to be their father."

"Why don't you come along and tell him yourself?" asked Darek.

Azzon shook his head. "Zahr would likely kill me before I got the words out. But if he will listen to you . . . if he will give me a chance . . . then I will come. Tell him to hoist a red flag from the main turret of the castle and I will come, alone and unarmed."

"What if he tricks you?" asked Darek. "What if he flies the flag and then kills you?"

Azzon looked down. "If he wants me dead," he said, "even knowing how I love him, then so be it."

Darek nodded slowly. "I will deliver your message," he said. He slipped the ring onto his thumb, then turned to Pola and Rowena.

"Give me two days," he said, "no matter *what*

happens, unless you know with certainty that I am dead. Do not come for me until then."

Pola and Rowena nodded. "What of the other men?" asked Pola.

"Stall them," said Darek. "Tell them I'm talking with Zahr, trying to free the slaves peacefully. Without Zarnak to egg them on, I think they'll wait."

Pola and Rowena each reached out an arm. Darek clasped them both in a brotherhood shake.

"Lord Eternal go with you," said Pola and Rowena.

"And with you," Darek returned.

"Boo-boo," wailed Zarnak. He held up a bloodied little finger.

Darek winked at Pola and Rowena. "Keep an eye on the *kids,*" he said. "I'll be back as soon as I can."

12

_____

Zantor was flying strongly. The night air was warm and damp. They were out of the mists now and the lights of Krad flickered ahead. Darek had left his battle mask behind. He wouldn't need it in Krad. Besides, if things went badly, he didn't want it to fall into the wrong hands. Now that he was on his way, he was scared. Really scared. It was one thing to talk of bravery, another actually to be brave. More than anything he wanted to turn back the clock, just to be a child again, at home with his mother, father, and Clep. But the clock didn't go backward. And even if it did, how could he go back and turn a blind eye to truth, let the dragon quests go on, let men and dragons die for nothing? *An adventure's an adventure, all the way to the end.* Yes. This adventure had a life of its own now. Wherever it led, he must follow.

As the city loomed closer, Darek's heart beat faster. There was unusual activity in the streets. People milled about and torches blazed. The turrets of Castle Krad were torchlit, too. Before long an alarm sounded. Darek and Zantor had been spotted.

The streets quickly emptied and warriors poured onto the battlements of Castle Krad. The moonlight glinted off their armor as they hastened to fit arrows to their bows. But before the first arrow could loft into the air, Darek gave the command.

"Down, Zantor."

Zantor tilted his wings and circled down into the center of the castle courtyard. Warriors

poured into the courtyard from all sides. A forest of arrows pointed at Zantor. Darek looked up and saw a second tier of arrows aiming down from the battlements.

"Easy, Zantor," Darek murmured. "Stay calm. Stay still."

Darek stared around him at the sea of hostile faces.

"I come in peace," he shouted. "I come to bargain with Zahr."

Straight ahead, a great flight of steps went up to a set of huge double doors. These swung slowly open now, and a tall Kraden appeared. He wore a crown and a long red robe that billowed out behind him. He walked to the edge of the steps, then stopped and stared at Darek. Darek shivered. So this was the mighty Zahr. The resemblance to Azzon was striking, except that this man's features were hardened by hate. Suddenly Zahr threw his head back and laughed.

"A *boy!*" he shouted. "The Zorians send a *boy* to bargain with the mighty Zahr?"

Darek bristled. "I'm not *just* a boy," he said loudly. "I'm the boy who escaped from your dragon nurseries. I'm the boy who rescued the Zorian prisoners from your mines. *I'm the boy who stole your dragons*. I am Darek of Zoriac."

Zahr's smile faded. "Come forward," he said.

Darek stroked Zantor's neck. "Stay," he said.

Grrawwwk, came a sharp mind cry.

"I'll be okay," said Darek. "Just wait here." Then he slid down Zantor's back to the ground. The warriors parted and Darek walked between them and mounted the steps. As soon as he reached the top, Zahr nodded to his guards.

"Seize him," he said. Two men lunged and grabbed Darek. Instantly Zantor reared, but just as instantly Zahr responded.

"KILL THE DRAGON!" he bellowed.

"NO!" Darek screamed. He turned to Zantor and shouted, "FLY, ZANTOR! Fly back to the mountains!"

Zantor sprang into the air, but a volley of arrows followed him. Darek winced as he saw several hit their mark. Images of terror and pain flooded Darek's head. Zantor's wings missed a beat, and for a moment it looked like he would fall. But then he rose again and cleared the castle walls.

"After him!" boomed Zahr.

Hordes of soldiers streamed out of the courtyard in pursuit of the dragon. Darek closed his eyes and sent the strongest mind message he could. *Fly! Fly! Fly for all you're worth!*

Messages of fear and pain still crowded into Darek's head long after Zantor disappeared. But that was all right. As long as the messages kept coming, Zantor was alive.

And then, suddenly, they stopped.

13

Darek stood chained against a cold cell wall. His arms were drawn up over his head so tightly that his toes barely touched the floor. He'd been dangling like that for hours. Maybe days. He didn't know. He didn't care. He only cared about one thing. Zantor. Why wasn't he sending messages? Why wasn't he answering Darek's silent pleas?

The cell door banged open and someone strode in. Darek looked up. It was Zahr, and he had a whip in his hand.

"Well, well," he said. "Ready to talk?"

"What happened to my dragon?" asked Darek.

"I had him made into a wall hanging," said Zahr. His cold eyes glittered like ice.

"You're lying!" Darek spat. "He's still alive. I know he is!"

"Do you now?" Zahr pulled at his chin. "And just *how* do you know it?"

Darek swallowed hard. *Zantor,* he cried inside his head. *Zantor, answer me.* But no answer came.

Zahr threw his head back and laughed. "I'll tell you what happened to your dragon," he said. "But first you tell me why your friends stole mine."

Darek bit his lip.

"Tell me what they want!" Zahr bellowed.

"They want the slaves," Darek said. "All of them. And they don't care who they have to kill to get them."

Zahr chuckled. "I thought as much," he said. "Well, let them come."

Darek stared at him. "They've got the dragons," he said. "You don't stand a chance."

Zahr chuckled again. "You underestimate me," he said. "A rider has been sent to my brother. He will arrive with his armies and dragons at any moment."

"I thought your brother was your enemy," said Darek.

Zahr laughed. "Maybe so," he said, "but he knows if I fall, he'll be next." Then Zahr's eyes narrowed. "How do you know about my brother?" he asked.

"Your father told me," said Darek.

The color drained from Zahr's face.

"My father . . . is dead," he said.

"No," said Darek. "Your father lives—in a cave under the Black Mountains."

Zahr took a step back.

"That's a lie," he said. "He can't be alive."

"He can be, and he is," said Darek. "He asked me to give you his ring." Darek pulled the great ring from his thumb and held it out to Zahr.

Zahr gasped, then clutched the ring and turned away. But not before Darek saw the wetness in his eyes.

"How do I know you're telling the truth?" Zahr cried. "How do I know the Zynots didn't find this ring on my father's body and give it to you?"

"Your father told me many things," said Darek, "about you and Rebbe. How he used to pit you against one another when you were boys and make you fight. How he used to beat the loser and send him to bed without supper."

Zahr whirled. His eyes blazed.

"Yes," he said. "And the loser was always me. The smaller one. But not anymore. I'm Zahr now. King of Krad. Envy of all men!"

Darek shook his head. "I don't envy you," he said. "Your brother is your enemy. Your father lives in fear of you. What joy does your kingdom bring?"

Zahr sneered. "Joy?" he said. "What is joy? How can one miss what one has never known?"

"You can know it now, Zahr," said Darek quietly. "Your father asked me to tell you he's sorry."

Zahr snorted. "Sorry!" he said. "He's sorry I beat him, that's all. Sorry that I'm king now, and he is nothing."

"No," said Darek. "He's content to be nothing. He doesn't want to be king. But there is one thing that he wants."

"Ahh," said Zahr, "and what would that be?"

"A chance to be a real father to you and Rebbe."

Zahr stared at Darek for long moment, then slowly shook his head. "It's too late for that," he said. "I don't need him anymore."

"I don't believe you," said Darek.

"What do you know of me?" asked Zahr.

"I know . . . I think . . . that on the inside you're not so different from me," said Darek. "And I know I need my father. And I miss him."

Zahr turned away and stared out the window. After a long silence he asked, "What else did he say?"

"He said . . . he loves you."

Zahr whirled once more. "Now I know you're lying," he said. "My father *never* spoke those words to me. Never in my life."

"He is waiting to speak them now," said Darek. "All you need do is hoist a red flag from the highest turret. Then he will come, alone and unarmed. And he will tell you for himself."

14

Azzon looked regal in his royal robes. Zahr and
Rebbe stood on either side of him. Their sharp
features were gentled by smiles. Gazing out over
the cheering throng of newly freed slaves, they
looked almost kind. Darek shook his head in wonder. It was a powerful force—a father's love.

It was a glorious day. A day to rejoice. A mes-
senger had been sent back to Zoriac to free Darek's and Rowena's fathers and bring them to Krad
to work out the details of the peace settlement. It
would take time, Darek knew, but he couldn't

help feeling that this was the start of a bright new future for all—dragons, Zorians, Kradens, and, yes, even the little Zynots. Only one thing still worried Darek. Zantor. Darek still hadn't learned the dragon's fate. Zahr had told him that Zantor had been wounded, but that he had made it back to the Black Mountains. But then why were there still no mind messages? Darek had tried to find a moment to question Azzon, but Azzon had been busy with his sons since his arrival.

"Look! In the sky!" someone shouted.

Darek looked up. Two Great Blue dragons were winging their way down into the courtyard. Drizba and Typra! And they were bearing Pola and Rowena. The crowd parted to let them land. In spite of his worries, Darek smiled. Rowena slid out of her saddle and rushed into his arms.

"Oh, Darek!" she cried. "It's so wonderful!"

"Yes," said Darek, one eye still on the sky. "But where is . . ."

Suddenly Pola rushed up and clapped Darek on

the back. "You did it, my friend," he said. "You really did it!"

Darek smiled. "We all did it," he said. "But where is . . ."

Just then Darek heard a sound, a faint sort of hum. A faint sort of *thrummm!* He whirled and looked. There, peeking out of Drizba's pouch, was the tiny blue head of a newborn dragonling! Darek's mouth dropped open. But . . . that was impossible. Drizba was too young to mate.

"What is that?" Darek asked, pointing. The little creature had climbed out of the pouch and was approaching on wobbly legs.

"Didn't Azzon tell you?" asked Rowena.

"Tell me what?" asked Darek. His eyes were riveted on the baby dragon. Warm, joyful feelings were filling his mind. All at once he knew!

"Zantor!" he cried. He ran to the dragonling and swept it up. The tiny tongue flicked out and kissed his cheek. Tears of joy welled in Darek's eyes. He hugged the dragonling tight, too overwhelmed to speak. At last he turned to Rowena and asked, "How?"

Rowena smiled. "He was badly wounded when he got back to the mountains," she said. "Azzon said he wasn't going to live because his body was so large and his heart so weak."

"So Azzon gave him the youth potion," Pola put in. "It shrank him down to a size his heart could manage. It shrank his wounds, too. Now they're only pinpricks."

"So, he's going to be okay?" said Darek.

Rowena smiled. "Yes," she said, stroking the nubby little head. "He's been doing a lot of sleeping. But he's going to be just fine."

"There's only one problem," said Pola. "Azzon had to give him such a strong dose that the aging process was completely reversed."

"What does that mean?" asked Darek.

"It means he's going to have to grow up all over again," said Rowena. "Do you think you're ready to raise a baby dragon again?"

Darek thought back over all Zantor's exploits of the past year, then he laughed. "Hey," he said, looking into the dragon's wide green eyes, "an adventure's an adventure, all the way to the end. Isn't it, little Dragon King?"

Zantor snuggled happily in Darek's arms. *"Thrummm,"* he sang. *"Thrummm, thrummm, thrummm."*

About the Author

Jackie French Koller is the author of over two dozen award-winning books for children and young adults, including *Nickommoh!* (Atheneum), *The Promise* (Knopf), *One Monkey Too Many* (Harcourt), and *Mole and Shrew* (Random House).

The mother of three grown children, Ms. Koller wrote the first *Dragonling* book for her youngest son, Devin, because dragons were his "favorite animals, next to dogs." Jackie French Koller lives on a mountaintop in Western Massachusetts with her husband and two Labrador retrievers. Visit her and Zantor on-line at http://jackiefrenchkoller.com.

About the Illustrator

Judith Mitchell has been an illustrator for some time, and has drawn and painted mermaids, trolls, griffins, fairies, Martians, monsters and—dragons! Dragons are special; Zantor is her favorite. Judith lives in New York City, where there is the subway, and near the ocean in Maine, where she suspects there are sea serpents. She is married to the handsomest man in the world.